D0361430

Remo's turn . . .

"I think you intend to kill me."

The man sneered again. "That's right. But we can kill you quickly. Decently. Or we can kill you slowly and painfully. Like this."

He nodded and the two big men grabbed Remo's head in their hands and began to squeeze. The fat man with the snub-nosed gun giggled.

There was a flash of contempt and anger. Remo dropped the man to his hands, fast, before he could be held up. Into the kneecap of the black man went an elbow, driving the kneecap through the joint, spinning the body upside down so that he went crashing into the counter with a crack. Up into the groin went a single hard finger, crushing a testicle, and driving the man into the air and then back against a pyramid of red paint cans which caught the shocked body and surrendered, splaying cans across the floor.

The fat man tried to squeeze the trigger. He was still trying when his muscles stopped receiving signals. They stopped receiving signals because there was something wrong with the remnants of his spinal column. A whole vertebra was in his throat.

Remo Williams, also known as The Destroyer, was at work.

THE DESTROYER: DEATH CHECK

by
Richard Sapir and Warren Murphy

PINNACLE BOOKS • NEW YORK CITY

THE DESTROYER: DEATH CHECK

An original Pinnacle Books edition
published for the first time anywhere.

First printing, January, 1972
Second printing, April, 1972
Third printing, August, 1972

Printed in the U.S.A.

PINNACLE BOOKS, 116 East 27 Street, New York, N.Y. 10016

To Dawn,
Because.

CHAPTER ONE

It was a very fast killing.

Touch the needle to the left arm. Press your thumb in between the left bicep and the tricep to pump up the vein. Ah, there it is. Clear the air from the syringe. Then in. Full. Slowly push the plunger all the way.

Done.

Remove the needle and let him collapse back again beside the chess table where he had fallen moments before. His head cracked on the polished parquet floor, and the killer could not help wincing, even though a man with a splendid overdose of heroin needs no sympathy.

"You know, my dear," said the man with the needle. "Some people pay for this. I mean they actually pay to do this to themselves."

"You didn't have to do it that way. You could have given him to me first. I wanted him tonight."

She said this, staring directly at the killer's eyes, trying to get him to look at her instead of the man on the floor. She wore black mesh stockings, covered to the knees with deeply polished black boots. She wore lipstick the color of dried blood. That was all. She held a whip in her left hand and when she stamped her feet, her naked breasts quivered.

"Will you listen to me?" she demanded.

"Shhh," said the man, his hand on the wrist of the person on the floor. "Ahh, yes. He must be in ecstasy. This might not be a bad way to go when you really think of it. Shhh."

There was silence. Then the man said, "A very fast and efficient job. He's dead."

"He's dead and what about me? Have you given any thought to me?"

"Yes, my dear. Put your clothes on." The man who had once been known as Dr. Hans Frichtmann busied himself pressing the now-empty hypodermic needle into the dead man's left arm in three other spots, barely missing the fatal entry hole. When the body was found, the holes would show that it had taken the victim four tries to find the vein. An amateur. That would help to explain the massive overdose. Not perfect, but it might do.

The woman in the boots had not moved. Now she spoke. "How about . . . you know, you and me? Normal."

"You and me would not be normal." He fixed his pale blue eyes on her. "Get your clothes on and help me with this unfortunate."

"Shit," she said.

"I do not find your total Americanization becoming," he said coldly. "Dress." She tossed her head angrily and her rich black hair cascaded around her bare shoulders as she turned and walked away.

Well before dawn, they placed the body behind a desk in an office at the Brewster Forum, a non-profit organization described as "pursuing research into original

8

thought." It was the office of the director of security, and when the man had been alive, it had been his office.

The head fell forward onto the blotter and the syringe was carefully dropped beneath the right hand, whose knuckles momentarily swung inches above the pile of the carpeting, then settled—very still—above the needle.

"Ah, that's it. Good. Perfect," said the man.

"A shameful waste," added the woman, who now wore a smart tweed suit and a fashionable knit cap, pulled down tightly over her head.

"My dear. Our employers are paying us very well to procure for them the plan to conquer the world. This imbecile got in our way. His death, therefore, is no waste. It is simply a requirement of our profession."

"I still don't like it. I don't like the planets for tonight. There is a force playing against us."

"Rubbish," the man said. "Did you give him a person check?"

"Yes. Was it rubbish when they almost caught us? Was it rubbish when. . . ?" Her voice trailed off as they left the office.

But the person check had not been made. And under the collar of the highly starched shirt of the director of security were clothbound negatives, tightly stitched into place.

The late director of security had sewn them there the previous evening, in response to a vaguely anticipated feeling of danger. When he had finished, he returned the needle and thread to his wife's sewing cabinet, kissed her, told a white lie about an evening of entertainment and moving up in the world, double-checked to make sure his insurance policies were still in view on top of their dresser and left their small home with all the phony nonchalance

9

he could generate without running the risk of being obvious.

Peter McCarthy had planned to find out just what those negatives meant. In eighteen years on the job, a small cog in the federal investigative machinery, it was the first time he had ever felt that his work was important.

Eighteen years on the job, with the money and the benefits, and they were one of the first families on the block with a color television, and Jeannie got a new coat every year, and the kids were in parochial schools and the station wagon was almost paid for, and they had all taken a cruise to the Bahamas the year before. Hell, $18,000 a year plus the $4,000 tax-free supplement for Peter McCarthy whose final high school grade was a straight C. Nice going.

As he walked away from his house, he wondered if the business with the insurance policies was not unnecessarily melodramatic. After all, this would probably turn out to be just someone's sordid little hobby. Messy, but not really important. He felt exhilarated.

Later that night, when he rested his forearms on the arms of a chair, surveying an element of the latest move in a game strange to him, Peter McCarthy realized he had found something big. But it was too late.

When his body was found the next morning, it was taken quietly to a nearby government hospital, where a five-man team of federal pathologists performed an eight-hour autopsy. Another team went over McCarthy's personal effects with miscroscopic thoroughness, removing the lining from his jacket, unstitching all his clothes, dissecting his shoes, and, eventually, finding the negatives.

The autopsy report and the negatives were sent away for further analysis, to a mental institution on Long Island Sound. There the negatives were duly processed into prints, examined for their film type and source of development, then sent to another department for reproduction and programming, then to another department which sent them to another department which hand-delivered them finally to an office where a bitter-faced man sat with an abacus. The processing had taken two hours.

"Let's see them," the lemon-faced man growled. "Haven't seen stuff like this since college. Of course, in college, we never paid $1,900 a print either."

When he was through with the last of the twelve prints, each the size of a large magazine page, he nodded that the bearer could leave. "Have them processed small for carrying and destruction. Water soluble will do."

"The negatives, too?"

"No, just the prints. Get out."

Then the bitter-faced man drummed on the polished abacus beads and spun his high dark chair to face out toward Long Island Sound.

He watched the night on the sound, dark and trailing far away to the Atlantic he had crossed as a young man in the O.S.S. To the Atlantic on whose shores he was given a last assignment he did not like and had at first refused and still wondered about at moments like this.

Peter McCarthy was dead. Murdered, according to the autopsy. And the negatives. They confirmed those vague hints of trouble at Brewster Forum and as far as the United States was concerned, Brewster Forum was heavy. Very heavy.

He went through the pictures again in his mind, then suddenly spun away from the view of the darkness and the stars, and pushed a button on a metal panel set into the space where the desk ordinarily would have had a top drawer.

"Yes?" came a voice.

11

"Tell programming to give me a match on backgrounders attached to the pictures. Have the computer do it. I don't want anyone playing games. I'm the only one to see the matchups."

"Yes sir."

"I might add that if I hear of any of those pictures being used for entertainment, heads will roll. Yours in particular."

"Yes sir."

In fourteen minutes and thirty seconds at the click of the chronograph stopwatch, the pictures in numbered envelopes arrived attached to resumes in numbered envelopes.

"Leave," said the bitter-faced man, checking the number on the envelope containing a photograph of a pudgy, middle-aged man wearing a black cape and busy stroking away at a wild-eyed, dark-haired woman wearing only long stockings and boots.

He looked at the resume. "Yes, I thought so. He's a goddam homosexual. Dammit." He put the resume back in the envelope and the pictures back in their envelopes and sealed them all. Then he spun back to the darkness of Long Island Sound.

A dead operative. Trouble at Brewster Forum. Photographs of a homosexual male playing with an obviously naked woman.

Yes or no, he thought. Remo Williams. The Destroyer. Yes or no. The decision was his to make, the responsibility his to bear.

He thought once more of Peter McCarthy who had worked for the past eight years for a federal agency he did not even know existed. And now he was dead. His family would carry forever the shame of a man who died from a self-inflicted overdose of narcotics. McCarthy's country-

12

men would never know that he had died for duty. No one would ever care. Should a man be allowed to die that gracelessly?

Back to the desk. Press the commissary button.

"Yes sir. Sort of early for phoning," came the voice.

"It's late for me. Tell the fish man we need more abalone."

"I think we still have some left in the freezer."

"Eat it yourself if you want. Just place the order for more."

"You're the boss, Doctor Smith."

"Yes, I am." Harold W. Smith turned back to the sound. Abalone. A man could come to hate the smell of it if he knew what it meant.

CHAPTER TWO

His name was Remo and the gymnasium was dark with only speckles of light coming from the ceiling-high windows where minute paint bubbles had burst shortly after workmen had applied the first layer of black. The gym, formerly the basketball court of the San Francisco Country Friends' School, had been built to catch the late afternoon sun over the Pacific, and when the owner was told by the prospective tenant that he would rent it only if the windows were blackened, he showed some surprise. He showed more when told he was never to visit the gym while the occupant was there. But the rent money was good, so the paint went on the windows the next day. And as the owner had told the man: "I'll stay away. For that kind of money, it's no concern of mine. Besides what can you do in a gym that isn't legal nowadays. Heh, heh."

So naturally, one day he hid himself in the small balcony and waited. He saw the door open and the tenant come in. A half hour later, the door opened again and the tenant was gone. Now the strange thing was that the owner heard not one sound. Not the creak of a floor-board, not a breath, not anything but his own heartbeat. Only the sound of the door opening and the door closing, and that was odd because the Country Friends School Gym was a natural sound conductor, a place where there was no such thing as a whisper.

The man named Remo had known someone was in the balcony because, among other things, he had begun that day working on sound and sight. Ordinarily the water pipes and the insects proved adequate. But that day there had been heavy nervous breathing in the balcony—the snorting sort of oxygen intake of overweight people. So that day Remo worked on moving in silence. It was a down day anyway, between two of the innumerable alert peaks.

Today, on the other hand, was an up peak and Remo carefully locked the three doors on the gym floor and the one to the balcony. He had been on alert for three months now, ever since the study package had arrived at the hotel. There were no explanations. Just the reading material. This time it was Brewster Forum, some sort of think tank. Some sort of trouble brewing. But there had been no call yet for Remo.

Remo felt upstairs was not quite on top of things. All his training had taught him you do not peak every week. You build to a peak. You plan for a peak. You work for it. To peak every day just means that that peak gets lower and lower and lower.

Remo had been peaking every day for three months now, and his eyes adjusted to the darkness of the gymnasium just a little less easily. True, not down to the level of ordinary men or even, for that matter, people who saw well in the dark. But he was less than he should be, less than he was trained to be.

15

The gym smelled of a decade of dirty socks. The air felt dry and tasted like old dictionaries stored in late summer attics. Dust particles danced in the minute rays coming from the specks in the black paint. In the far corner where rotting ropes hung from the ceiling came the buzz of a fly.

Remo breathed, steadily, and relaxed the centrality of his being to lower the pulse and expand what he had learned was the calm within him. The calm which the European and especially the American European had forgotten, or perhaps never knew. The calm from which came the personal power of the human being—that power which had been surrendered to the machine which had apparently done things faster and better. The machine had lowered industrial man to the use of less than seven per cent of his abilities, compared to the nine per cent average for primitives. Remo remembered the lecture.

At his peak, Remo—who eight years before had been officially executed in an electric chair for a crime he did not commit, only to be revived to work for an organization that did not exist—at his peak, this man Remo could use nearly half the power of his muscles and senses.

Forty five to forty eight per cent or, as his main instructor had said, "a moment of just more darkness than light." This poetic phrase had been translated for upstairs into a maximum operating capacity of 46.5 plus or minus 1.5.

Now Remo could feel the dark in the gym grow heavier as the peak descended day by day. One had to laugh. So much effort, so much money, so much danger in even setting up the organization, and now upstairs the only two officials in the country who knew exactly what he did were ruining him. Faster than Seagrams Seven and Schlitz chasers, without as much fun.

16

·The organization was CURE. It did not appear in any government budget nor in any report. The outgoing President verbally told the next incoming President.

He showed him the scrambler phone where he could reach the head of CURE, and then later, as they smiled to the world from the back seat of a limousine headed to the inauguration, confided:

"Now, don't you fret none about that group I was tellin' you about yesterday. They do everything real quiet and only two of 'em know what in a cow's ass they're doing.

"It's just that a crooked prosecutor'll be discovered by some newspaperman who just happens to get some damaging information. Or some evidence'll turn up during a trial and the D.A. will win one that was going down the chute. Or someone who you'd just never think would *goes* and turns state's evidence and testifies. It's just the extra little edge to make things more workable."

"I don't like it," whispered the President-elect, flashing his famous plastic smile to the crowds. "It if turns out publicly that the United States government is violating the very laws that make it the United States government, right then and there you might as well admit our form of government is inoperable."

"Well, I ain't saying nothin'? Are you?"

"Of course not."

"Well, what's the problem?"

"I just don't like it. How would I stop this thing?"

"You just make a phone call and the two men who know about it retire."

"That phone call in some way sets off something or someone who kills them, doesn't it."

"I 'spect so. They got more safeguards on this thing than Uncle Luke's still. Look, there are two things you

17

can do with this group. Let it do whatever it does. Or stop it. That's all."

"But you did say I could suggest assignments?"

"Yup. But they're chock full anyhow. And anyway, they only take the kind of stuff that either endangers the constitution or that the country can't handle any other way. Sometimes, it's fun figuring out just which things they're involved in and which things they ain't. You get pretty good at it after awhile."

"I was thinking last night what if the man who runs this group decides to take over the country?"

"You always got the phone."

"Suppose he plots the murder of the President?"

"You're the only one who can OK the use of the one person who would do it. The other man who knows about that outfit. Just one man. That's the safeguard. Hell, I know you're shocked. You shoulda seen my face when the head of this group got a personal visit with me. The President didn't tell me a thing before he was shot. Just like you won't tell your vice president." He turned and smiled at the crowds. "Especially yours."

He smiled a creased smile and nodded solemnly to the people on his side of the car. The Secret Service bodyguards puffed alongside.

"I was thinking last night, what if the head of this organization dies?"

"Damned if I know," said the Texan.

"Frankly, this revelation frightens me," said the President-elect, raising his eyebrows, head and hands as though just spotting a close friend in a crowd of strangers. "I haven't felt at ease since you told me about it."

"You can stop it anytime," the Texan responded.

"That one man they've got must be pretty good. The one who goes on the assignments, I mean."

18

"I don't know for sure. But from what that little feller told me that day, they don't just use him for wrapping up garbage."

"Let me make one thing perfectly clear. I don't like this whole business."

"We didn't ask you to take office," said the Texan with a smile.

So Remo Williams stood silently in the gymnasium feeling his conditioning leave him. He breathed deeply, then slid through the dark, in almost imperceptible movements, and was in the balcony. He wore black tennis shoes so that he could not see his feet, a tee shirt dyed black so that the white of the shirt in the dark would not throw off unbalancing brightness. His shorts were black. Night moving in night.

He moved from the balcony rail to the top of the basketball backboard. He seated himself carefully, with his right hand between his legs and his legs stretched out over the hoop below. Funny, he thought. When he was a policeman in his twenties, he would have been puffing if he ran a block, and probably would have had to engineer a desk job by thirty five or face a heart attack. It was nice then. Just walk into any bar you wanted when off duty. Have a pizza for supper if you wished. Get laid when you had a chance.

But that was when he was alive. And when he was officially alive, there were no such things as peak periods with rice and fish and abstinence. Actually, he didn't really have to follow the regimen. He thought about that often. He could probably do very well at less than full capacity. But a wise Korean had told him that deterioration of the body is like a stone rolling down a mountain. So easy to start, so hard to stop. And if Remo Williams couldn't stop, he would be very dead.

He lowered his shoes to the rim, getting the feel of its grip into the backboard. If you know the feel of objects, the feel of their mass, their movement and their strength, you could use that as your strength. That was the secret of force. To not fight it. And to not fight it was the best way to fight people when you had to.

Remo stood up on the rim and gathered the where of the floor into his balance. He should have changed the height of the hoop, because sooner or later he would be performing muscle memory instead of proper use of balance and judgment. When he had first learned the exercise, he watched a cat for a day and a half. He had been told to become the cat. He had answered that he would prefer to become a rabbit so he could get laid, and how long was this dingaling training going to go on?

"Until you are dead," he was told.

"You mean fifty years."

"It might be fifty seconds, if you are not good enough," said the Korean instructor. "Watch the cat."

And Remo had watched the cat and for a few moments thought, *really* thought, he could become the cat.

Now Remo Williams indulged his own private little joke which signalled the start of the exercise.

"Meow," he whispered in the silent, dark gym.

He stood on the rim, straight up, and then his body fell forward, shoes gripping the rim by pressure, head going forward, shoes flipping up, rim adding force, body heading straight down, hair and head aiming straight at the floor—like a dark knife dropping into a dark sea.

His hair touched the varnish of the floor and triggered a body trunk flip, the dark form in the blackened gym spinning in space, the sneakers coming around quick—rocket fast—arching and down steady standing on the wooden floor.

20

Blat. The sound echoed in the gymnasium. He had held for the last hair-touching instant and then let the muscles take over, the muscles of a cat which shifted the body in air and put the feet on the floor. An exercise the body could do only when the mind was trained, trained to steal the balance of another animal.

Remo Williams had heard the blat in the gym, the sound of his sneakers hitting the floor. He was not purring.

"Shit," he mumbled to himself. "The next time it'll be my head. That dumb bastard is gonna get me killed yet, with his goddam peak period."

And he returned to the balcony and the backboard, this time to do it right. Without a sound when his sneakers hit the floor.

CHAPTER THREE

The sun reflected on the scales of the fish and played on the water and warmed the covered wood pier of Giuseppe Bresicola's wholesale fish market which jutted out into San Francisco Bay like dirty toy sticks on a blue plate.

Bresicola's did not smell of fish: it breathed of fish and sounded of fish, from the splat of mackerel piled on mackerel to the scrape of steel across scales. Entrails in giant barrels in seconds began the inevitable decay. Fresh seawater squooshed over the scale-caked wood. And Bresicola smiled because his friend was again visiting him.

"I no tella you the orders today, Mr. Time-Study man. Not today." He made a playful stab at his friend's head. How nice this boy moved. Like a dancer. Like Willie Pep. "You don't get the orders today."

"What do you mean, not today," asked the friend who was six feet tall and husky. He scraped his brown shoes playfully on the wood, a small dance without motion. They were good shoes, $50 shoes. Once he had bought ten pairs of $100 shoes and then heaved them out into the

Bay, but the next day all he did was draw money from his account and buy new shoes. So, he had gotten that out of his system and throwing shoes away meant only that you had to take the trouble of buying more.

"It's abalone," said Bresicola. "We got another order from New York. Just now."

"So?"

"So the last time I tell you about abalone, I no see you for a month."

"You think abalone has something to do with my work here?"

"You think maybe Giuseppe is stupid, Mr. Time-Study man?"

"No. Many people are stupid. Especially back east. But not you, paisan. Not you."

"It's something maybe to do with the stock market, yes?"

"If I said yes, you wouldn't believe me."

"I believe anyting you say. Anyting."

"It's the stock market."

"Not for a minute does Giuseppe believe that."

"I thought you said you'd believe me?"

"Only if you makea sense. Stock market makea no sense."

"Abalone makes no sense? Time studies make no sense?"

"Nothing makes no sense," Bresicola insisted.

Very good, thought the time study man, because now was no time to be giving out signals. It would be a very nice way to get oneself killed. First, loss of your vibrations, then your awareness, then your balance, and before long, you were just a normal, cunning, strong human being. And that would not be enough. Not nearly enough.

He shared with Bresicola a glass of sharp red wine,

made plans for dinner with no definite date, and when he left, had decided it was long past time to eliminate the time-study man.

He would exist until a plane ticket had been purchased with his American Express card and until $800 in travelers' checks were cashed. He would exist all the way from San Francisco to Kennedy Airport in New York City. He would walk into the men's room closest to the Pan American counter, look for a pair of blue suede shoes indicating that the wearer was reposing on the commode, wait till the room was clear, then mention that the urinals never worked and that he hoped some day the Americans could learn plumbing from the Swiss.

A wallet would come out from under the closed commode door and the time-study man's wallet would go in as exchange. The man inside would not open the door to see who got the wallet. He had been told that to open the door was to lose his job. There was even a better reason. If he should even glimpse the man who got the wallet, he would lose his life.

Remo Williams flipped the time-study man's wallet into the hand coming from beneath the door and snatched the other wallet in a motion so fast the person in the commode only knew there had been a switch by the change in the shade of the leather.

So much for the time-study man. Remo Williams left the men's room for a small cocktail lounge on the second level, from which he could look back down to make sure the blue suede shoes left the terminal without looking around.

The bar was dark, hiding the afternoon, a perpetual womb, a dispenser of nerve killers that Remo Williams was not allowed to have because he was on peak. He ordered ginger ale, then checked the wallet.

24

The seals were unbroken. He checked the credit cards and the wallet flap for the needle he had been assured would bring instant death. With the credit cards was a small card with phone numbers that were not phone numbers. By adding the numbers in the series, Remo learned that:

1) The Reach-Me-Urgent was the same. A Chicago dial-a-prayer. (That would have to be changed because of deteriorating phone service.)

2) The next training checkout with Chiun, his Korean teacher, was scheduled six weeks later at Plensikoff's Gym on Granby Street, Norfolk, Va. (Dammit, Chiun could stay alive long.)

3) The assignment meeting was at the Port Alexandria at 8 p.m., a face-to-face, with—oh no—Harold W. Smith himself.

4) He was now Remo Pelham. A former policeman. Born and raised in the Bronx. DeWitt Clinton High School, where he remembered only the football coach, Doc Wiedeman, who would not remember him. An M.P. in Vietnam. Chief of industrial security at a Pittsburgh mill. No family. No furniture, but books and clothes would be arriving in two days at Brewster Forum, which had just named him director of security at $17,000 per year.

He scanned the sheet and committed it to memory. Then he folded it up and dropped it into the remnants of his ginger ale. In ten seconds, it had dissolved, making the drink murky. It had been the intention of someone that Remo should be able to dispose of the paper by swallowing it. There were two reasons he would not swallow it—one, it tasted like glue; two, he didn't swallow things sent to him by anyone.

He took a cab into New York City with a woman who

didn't like New York City, didn't know why she was visiting it and would never visit it again. So many people with only one thing on their minds. Not like Troy, Ohio. Had Mr. Pelham heard of Troy, Ohio?

"Yes, I know Troy, Ohio," said Remo Pelham. "It has an intelligence quotient of two hundred. That's cumulative for everyone."

Mr. Pelham did not have to be insulting. Mr. Pelham might have told her he was from New York City instead of becoming abusive. After all, she was sure not everyone in New York City had only one thing on their minds.

Mr. Pelham informed the woman he was born in the Bronx and took to heart things said about New York City. He loved his home town.

Mrs. Jones loved New York City also, she was only teasing and what hotel was Mr. Pelham staying at?

"Not sure yet. I'm going to Riverside Drive."

"Is it pretty?"

Remo turned to the woman for closer scrutiny. He should get rid of her. Now he was deciding whether he wanted to.

She was a full-bodied woman with strong clean features, a blonde with brown eyes under heavy blue eyeshadow. She wore a neat suit, whose sewing and material Remo estimated at $250 in a large Cleveland store or $550 in New York City. The ring was three karats—if flawless, a fine stone.

The shoes oozed the subtle richness of expensive leather. Wife of manufacturer or leading citizen, on shopping trip to New York, and if convenient, uncomplicated lay for herself.

Estimating clothes and accoutrements had been one of his poorer programs during training. But he was good enough to trust himself. As much as indicating wealth,

26

clothes tell you what a person wants you to believe. Invariably, that could give you a handle.

Remo Pelham answered the question: "Riverside Drive overlooks the Hudson. It's pretty."

"Where on Riverside, Mac?"

"Anywhere," Remo told the driver.

"You, too, lady?"

"If I wouldn't be bothering anyone," she said.

Remo Pelham said nothing. He said nothing as he paid the driver at 96th Street and Riverside Drive and got slowly out of the cab. He did not turn around nor offer to help the woman with her luggage.

Remo Pelham did not need luggage. Neither did a half dozen other names he lived by. He walked to the low stone wall and stared out across the Hudson, glimmering in the hot September day.

Across that river and beyond the decaying docks of Hoboken, in the city of Newark, a young policeman had been tried, found guilty of murder and executed at the state penitentiary. A young policeman who swallowed a pill from a priest who had offered last rites and promised him not eternal life, but life. He had taken the pill, passed out in the electric chair, and awakened to hear a story from a man with a hook for a hand. The story was this:

The American constitution didn't work and was working less each year. Criminals, using the safeguards of the constitution, daily increased in number and strength. The next step was a police state. Machiavelli's classic perception of chaos and then repression.

Should the government scrap the constitution? Or allow the country to come apart? There was a third choice. Suppose an organization outside the government evened the odds? An organization which could not transcend the constitution because the organization would never exist?

27

If it never existed, who could say the constitution didn't work? And when the odds were more even, the organization which did not exist would quietly close shop. Closing shop would be very easy. Only four people knew for sure what CURE did—the highest elected official; Harold W. Smith, who was the operations head; Conrad MacCleary, the man with the hook who was the recruiter and now, the latest addition, the young policeman Remo Williams who had officially died the night before in an electric chair.

It was the high elected official who had given the go-ahead for what Remo would do. What he would do was kill. When all else failed, he would kill.

"But why me?" Remo had asked.

"A lot of things," MacCleary, the recruiter, had answered. "I saw you in operation in Nam. According to a shrink who didn't know why he was testing young policemen, you have a compulsion to mete out punishment, a vengeance fixation, he called it. Frankly, I think he's a bag of wind. I want you becuase I've seen you move."

It was a good explanation. Incredibly complex training followed at the hands of Chiun, an aged Korean, who could kill with a fingernail and in whose parchment hands anything became a lethal weapon. And then Remo saw the man with the hook again. He saw him dying and he had orders to kill him.

That had been eight years ago and now he didn't even have an old jacket. Everything was new; nothing had worth. The Hudson breathed its stink of civilization out into the Atlantic, a giant sewer from a civilization that made everything a sewer.

"It certainly is a lovely river," said the woman.

"Lady," said Remo Pelham, "you've got taste up your ass."

As he began to walk away, she shrieked, "What about my luggage? You can't leave me here with this luggage. I came with you. You're the man! *You've got to do something about this luggage.*"

And Remo took care of the luggage, a large heavy suitcase and a small modeling box, by flipping them over the dark stone wall to the West Side Highway forty yards below where they burst on the roof of a passing Cadillac.

CHAPTER FOUR

The bitter-faced man sat just beyond the spotlight's reach, his legs crossed, his left elbow on the small round table, his right hand resting in the crook of the opposite elbow. He wore a gray suit, white shirt and gray tie. His rimless glasses occasionally reflected the light as did his precision combed hairline with its micrometer-straight part.

He did not move from this position for fifteen minutes, not when the voluptuous dancer strained in sweaty ecstasy against the confines of her beads, or when joyful enthusiasts threw dollar bills onto the floor or stuffed them in her jeweled breast cups. Smoke curled to the ceiling. Sweets-loaded trays hovered over the heads of scurrying waiters. The plinking excitement of the bouzoukis caught the audience in its rhythms and joys and shrieks of life. The man did not move.

One man moved, almost floating through the dark crowd to the table of the bitter-faced man.

30

"You're as obvious as a bowl of garbage in Tiffany's," said the man known as Remo Pelham.

"Good to see you. I want to congratulate you on your selection as director of security for Brewster Forum."

"You're sitting here like a stone. Don't you think someone might wonder what a man who acts like an embalmer is doing in the Port Alexandria? Isn't it obvious you're here to meet someone?"

"So what?"

"So look as if you're having some fun. After all, aren't we playing the sex-frustrated executive who frequents places like this for voyeuristic thrills?"

"Something like that. Even better, the noise levels here have been checked out."

"You don't look like a voyeur," Remo insisted. "You aren't even interested in the women."

"I'm interested in getting out of here. Now listen—Dammit, why the hell do I have so much trouble with you? Listen." Smith leaned forward as a new dancer came center floor to heavy applause.

"You look upset."

"I am. Listen. You will meet a man on the Staten Island ferry leaving the Battery at 11 a.m. tomorrow. He will be wearing a blue and red striped tie and carrying a gray wrapped package the size of a briefcase. It's heavy because it's a water case around water soluble documents. Pictures and biographies. You can get the documents out dry using the Oriental string puzzle Chiun says you know."

"How is Chiun?"

"Dammit, will you listen?"

"Will you tell me how Chiun is?"

"He's fine."

"He was worried about his arteries."

31

"I don't know about his arteries. He's always fine. Now listen. Major point. Brewster Forum is of utmost importance to the country, maybe the world. Your predecessor was one of ours at a low level. He was murdered, even though it was covered as a suicidal overdose of heroin. He stumbled onto something."

"What?"

"We're not sure. Pornographic photos of the top staff at the forum. The photos are genuine. But still the whole thing doesn't ring true. You'll see that when you meet the staff. And check resume four against pictures 10, 11, and 12."

"It doesn't sound like it's in my line," Remo said.

Smith ignored the interuption. "Ordinarily, we'd suspect blackmail. But that doesn't cut either. Why would a blackmailer be working on the whole staff at Brewster Forum? There are other wealthier, more obvious, victims. No, there's something more to it."

"It still doesn't sound like it's in my line."

Smith looked up into Remo's placid brown eyes. "Don't misunderstand. Brewster Forum is very, very important."

He leaned forward conspiratorially. "A plan to conquer the world. You'll see on a transcript that's with the photos. My superior doesn't want that work stopped. But if it's going to be stopped, we'll do the stopping. That's you. If you can find out who's responsible for the sex photos, well and good. If you can straighten out that mess without harm to the Forum's work, even better. But your mission is to set up the deaths of every one of the top staff at Brewster Forum, either as a group or individually, on a one-hour call if necessary. No misses. Death as an absolute certainty."

Remo interrupted. "I read something like this once. We're going to destroy them in order to save them?"

"Don't get cute," Smith said. "Whatever it is they're working on there, my superior is worried about an enemy getting his hands on it. Someone might be planning to blackmail our government. That could explain those photos. It would make them worth a bundle. But other agencies are planning to deal with the photos. We just want to be ready to move in case they come up empty, and the Forum is endangered."

"How much time do I have?"

"We don't know. We think we bought some time because McCarthy, he was the security director, came up with the negatives. If those photos are really tied in with this, it might mean they have to all be done over. That would have to take a while. By the way. . . ."

"I know what 'by the way' means."

"By the way. When you get your package from the man on the ferry, he will probably want to talk to you. Ask you about your job. You might even be attacked. If you are, you know what to do."

"Yes, I know what to do. I also know that you have a nasty little habit of cleaning house everytime you give me a go-ahead. Who is the guy?"

"None of your business."

"Maybe I'll just take the package."

"Maybe you will. When you see him, mention that you intend to take up photography because you know you could take great pictures of New York's skyline."

"Right. Now let me give you a 'by the way.' I'm just taking the package."

"You could do us a lot of good."

Remo leaned back and smiled, letting his brown eyes roam from the voluptuous figure, glistening and writhing in rhythm on the floor to the very stiff, unusually tense for a non-budget month, Harold W. Smith, operational head of CURE.

"Put a dollar in her bra."

"What?," said Smith.

"Put a dollar in her bra."

"I will not."

"You will."

"You mean to tell me that other things depend upon your gratification from embarrassing me?"

"By the way, I don't know." Remo grinned.

"All right. A dollar, you said."

Remo watched Smith take a dollar from his wallet and, holding it like a live bug, extend it out over the dance floor. The woman, whose milky skin glistened from perspiration, shimmy shouldered over beneath the dollar and Smith dropped it, then turned quickly back to the table pretending he had never been involved in anything so sordid. The bill lay on the throbbing pink-white mountains.

"Stuff it in."

"I will not."

"All right. Goodbye."

"All right."

"Five dollars."

"Five. Now see here. . . ."

"Five."

"All right. Five. You just love to spend money."

Smith crinkled a five-dollar bill in his hands, and with a get-it-over-fast speed leaned down to the woman who came up to meet his money with her bosom. He did not see his companion also reach forward with money, and under the cover of this motion slip a hand behind the jeweled breast cups and snap the metal holding band, flipping the bra, cups and all around Smith's hand.

34

The breasts ballooned out. Smith gasped. The crowd cheered. The woman swung at Smith's head, reaching for her bra.

"We could lose our license, you dumb fuck," she screamed, scoring again on the forehead of one of the most powerful men in the country, who desperately tried to hold on his glasses while trying to leave the table.

And the man known as Remo Pelham floated to the door, telling everyone he passed, "You never know by the looks. You never know. Shocking what these degenerates will do."

CHAPTER FIVE

The package bearer might very well have lived out the afternoon. He might even have saved his colleague's lives. Certainly there was no danger from the man who mentioned his love for photography and New York City skylines.

But the man with the gray package said something. With a sneer, he said: "We know what's in the water package. And we know we can't open it. So you're going to open it for us. Do you know why you're going to open it for us?"

"No," said Remo, lying. He had seen the two big men, one black and the other white, pretending to lounge on the seats behind them. "Beautiful skyline, don't you think?" He breathed deeply of the almost breathable air between Staten Island and New York City.

"You are going to open the package because you want to save your life. Look behind you."

"And leave the beauty of the gulls and the twin towers

of the trade center, the Empire State Building? My little island in the sun?"

Remo did a little semi-pushup against the second deck railing of the ferry and watched the white churning swirls bubble out back toward Manhattan. Then he felt two strong arms on each of his arms. He looked again at the man with the gray package and the sneer and said:

"You're not going to believe this. But I'll give you all a chance to live."

The man did not believe this. The man believed he was talking to a prankster.

So the man who cared about photography went with the large men and the man with the package to a paint store on Staten Island. The store was closed that day, but it was opened for them by a fat man. With a gun.

The man who loved photography tried. He said: "Look. You're just a messenger. You give the package to me. I'm just a messenger. I give it to someone else. Why should we fight over it?"

The man with the package sneered again. "You're wrong all around. I'm not just your messenger. He met with an accident. You are not just a messenger. I was informed otherwise. It seems you lose."

"Last chance to reconsider," Remo said.

"Sorry," said the other. "We'll have to risk it."

Remo registered the moves of his four adversaries. The two big men were obviously in condition; he had felt how light they were on their feet when they walked him off the ferry. The man with the package had been in condition once. The short man who had opened the door was very fat and had never been in condition. But he made up for it. He carried a snub-nosed revolver. A snub-nosed revolver is good for one thing. Close work. What it loses in accuracy, it gains in compactness. It's not easy to reach out,

37

grab the barrel and the cylinder, and smother the falling hammer, all in one motion.

The two big men stayed behind Remo as the man put the gray package down on the counter. The fat man stayed near the shuttered door.

"Well," said the man who had held the package.

"This is the package and not an imitation?"

"This is the package."

"If it's an imitation, I can get hurt."

"It is the package."

"These things tend to explode."

"Open it."

Remo carefully removed the clear tape from the tips of the gray package. Through the holes in the corners protruded four knots of thin red string. The knots were symmetrical. As Remo looked at them, deeply, with his mind free, he could almost feel the inner harmony of the man who had tied them. It was the real package. Chiun had tied the knots.

"Something wrong, Pelham?"

"How did you know my name was Pelham?"

"Untie the package."

"How did you know my name was Pelham?"

"Untie the package and I'll tell you."

"I think you intend to kill me."

The man sneered again. "That's right. But we can kill you quickly. Decently. Or we can kill you slowly and painfully. Like your messenger. Like this."

He nodded and the two big men grabbed Remo's head in their hands and began to squeeze. The fat man with the snub-nosed gun giggled. The man with the package watched, waiting to see pain and surrender in the victims' eyes.

But there was no surrender. Only a flash of contempt

38

and anger. The man dropped to his hands, fast before he could be held up. Into the close kneecap of the black man went an elbow, driving the kneecap through the joint, spinning the body upside down so the Afro went crashing into the counter with a crack. Up into the white man's groin went a single hard finger, crushing a testicle and driving the man into the air and then back against a pyramid of red paint cans which caught the shocked body and surrendered, splaying cans across the floor.

The fat man tried to squeeze the trigger. He was still trying when his muscles stopped receiving signals. They stopped receiving signals because there was something wrong with the remnants of his spinal column. A whole vertebra was in his throat.

The two big men were retching on the floor. The man who had held the package just gasped. When he saw the now-hard brown eyes stare into his mind and feed upon his fear, when he suddenly smelled his own death upon him, he urinated.

"How did you know my name was Pelham?"

"I was told."

"By someone at Folcroft?"

"I never heard of Folcroft."

"Who told you?"

The man had edged away from the package along behind the paint store counter. Now he said calmly, "There's a man behind you with a gun."

The man was a pro. He could suffer a setback, regain his composure, then try a very old trick that almost always worked. The trick assumed that the person it was used on was so engrossed in the tension of the conversation that he had shut off his perception of other things.

This was true of most people. But most people had not stood for hours in empty gymnasiums, dodging three

39

swinging knives, suspended by ropes from the ceiling, while being expected to yell out how many doors behind them opened and closed when they opened and closed. When practiced, enough, this indelibly trained the perception so that it took a conscious act of will to turn it off. It did not turn off during tension. But how was the man behind the counter to know it?

He was so terribly involved with the gun he was bringing up from behind the counter that he just assumed the trick would work. He knew it would not when his wrist ceased to function and he lost consciousness.

Remo permanently ended the convulsions of the two athletes. Then he placed the fat man behind the counter where he belonged. He lifted all three of their wallets. He was taking the wallet from the pocket of the man with the package when the man stirred. Remo had another question: "What happened to the messenger?"

The man was no longer afraid of death since it had, he knew, become inevitable. "I killed him. I shot his eyes out. I enjoyed it." He sneered.

Remo reached down and squeezed his broken wrist, hard enough to feel one broken bone skid against another. With a shriek, the man passed out again.

When the man came to a few minutes later, his head hurt more than his wrist. His eyes bulged in horror as he realized that his head was squeezed top and bottom between the two metal plates of an electric paint-mixing machine. Out of the corner of his eye, he saw Remo toss the "on" switch. Then he felt his head separate from his neck and he never saw anything again.

Remo looked back over the scene. A paint store owner was robbed and brutally attacked. A passerby who tried to stop the robbery had his head locked in the paint mixer. Okay. Then who killed the two robbers? Who stole their wallets? To hell with it. Let the *Daily News* figure it out. They were good at that sort of thing.

Remo picked up the gray box, stuffed the four dead men's wallets into his raincoat pocket and locked the door behind him.

He stopped at a stationery store, brought a strip of brown wrapping paper, and made a package of the four wallets. He addressed it to Dr. Harold W. Smith, Folcroft Sanitarium, Rye, New York, and mailed it at a small branch post office.

Smith read the papers. He would know what corpses had surrendered the wallets. Remo would find out later who they were.

On the ferry back to New York City, two nine-year-old twin boys going bang-bang with their fingers were given a snub-nosed .38 and a .32 caliber Smith and Wesson— both cartridge free—to play with.

When their shocked mother inquired where the two boys had gotten the guns, they couldn't really describe the man.

"He was nice and—I don't know—he was just a grownup."

"Yeah. He was a real grownup, Mommy."

CHAPTER SIX

When Remo saw the first picture, he began to chuckle. Then laugh. Then guffaw, then shake so hard he almost dropped the whole package into the wet motel sink where he had unravelled the strings according to instructions taught him years before.

Under a half-page biography of Dr. Abram Schulter, M.D., Ph.D., fellow of the American College of Surgeons, Diplomate of the American Neurological Society, Nobel Laureate, pioneer in brain surgery, was a photograph of Doctor Schulter in action.

He was nude, a frail man with a big, happy grin, fornicating with a dark haired girl. Strapped to his back, and just as obviously mounting him, was a toy giraffe, the large furry type children like to pretend they are riding.

Doctor Schulter was smiling as if he had realized something very funny. Perhaps, thought Remo, that he loved the giraffe more.

The two other pictures showed Doctor Schulter: A)

mounting the toy with the girl mounting him; B) mounted by the toy which was mounted by the girl.

The biography continued: "Doctor Schulter. Foremost authority on brain waves. Married 20 years, two children, active in Professional Societies, American Art Association, National Disturbed Children Foundation. No serious political connections. Top security clearance."

Then Remo went though the other pictures and biographies.

Dr. Anthony J. Ferrante, an expert in bio-feedback, whatever the hell that was, stood in a karate shirt minus the karate pants. He did not need the pants to protect his modesty because there was a girl in the camera's way. On her knees. Apparently the same girl who had been teaching the neurosurgeon the secrets of the giraffe was now demonstrating a different kind of secret to Dr. Ferrante. Doctor Ferrante was demonstrating to the camera a karate blow. His face was dark and intent. Karate, thought Remo, can be serious business.

Dr. Robert Boyle, a bio-cycle analyst, liked the plain old missionary position. This was not surprising since Doctor Boyle was a Jesuit priest.

Dr. Nils Brewster, distinguished head of Brewster Forum and author of the famous "Dynamics of Peace, the study of aggression and containment," discovered a new level of containment. He was dressed in chains.

Dr. James Ratchett, biochemist, was dressed formally. In a top hat, black cape and bare front. He was being whipped by the black-haired girl who appeared in all the pictures. Two other photos showed Ratchett making it with the girl. He had dropped the cape and still visible across his back were the angry pouting welts of the whip.

But on Doctor Ratchett's biography was a hand-written note. It was Smith's handwriting.

43

"Dr. Ratchett is a notorious homosexual."

Remo went through the photographs three times. The chuckles had dwindled to boredom by the end of the first round. The girl was the same in each picture. Remo regretted his only cursory knowledge of photography, but the pictures looked extremely well lighted and posed, as though a fine fashion photographer had played the scene for drama—highlights, explosive beams, shadows.

These were the great minds America would rather see dead than. . . . Than what? Smith had said he did not know than what?

Remo set the photos out in rows on the brown tile motel sink. He opened his eyes wide, then splashed his eyes along the rows of photographs, blinking rapidly, turning his eyes and brain into a giant stroboscopic system, registering every detail, every shadow indelibly on his brain. He performed the exercise twice, to be sure he had missed nothing. Done. He had been peaked too long. Ordinarily, once would have been enough.

Smith's words repeated themselves to Remo as he dropped the pictures into the motel washbasin, holding a last typewritten sheet which was a transcription of a conversation. Smith had told him:

"All we know is something is wrong. We can't, under any circumstances, allow these people's efforts to be used by any other power. We don't even know yet if whoever is producing these pictures is international or criminal. We just don't know. We do know that we want these scientists' abilities to be denied at a moment's notice to whoever is doing whatever the hell is going on there. That means they must be eliminated on command. And that means you must set them up."

And other words came back to Remo: "Stupidity is a function of mankind, ignorance the beginning of wisdom,

44

wisdom the knowledge of ignorance." That was Chiun, his instructor.

Chiun always had a bit of wisdom that didn't seem to mean anything, until one day you needed it. Now it meant something.

He had been kept at peak alert for three months while CURE attempted to figure out what it was protecting, and with the first sign that it was in danger, they sent in their weapon to be able to destroy it on command.

"Brilliant," Remo said to himself, running water into the sink. He watched the photographs become white, then separate, then dissolve and turn the water in the sink to milk. "Brilliant."

And he played with an idea he played with almost every month. Running. He could never be a cop again, he had no past. But he might be able to get into the Teamsters or even into a job where no one cared about the past. Maybe a salesman. Maybe open a store somewhere after clipping CURE for a bundle. A store. A wife. A family. A home.

And then one day he would lift a car off a person, or settle a dispute in a bar and do it just a mite too well, and CURE would find him. And that would be that, because by then there would be another just like him and if that person came delivering the mail or the milk, Remo would be dead. If a thinking man wants to get you badly enough, he will get you. How few people realized their vulnerability ... well, why should they? No one was after them.

And so the pictures were now liquid and Remo Williams pulled the plug and let them go down the drain where they would wash into sewers and then rivers, and then never be seen again. Lucky fucking pictures.

Remo read the transcript. "A conversation between A

and B two years ago. B is another agency, same team. A is the head of XXX."

Even in a water seal envelope, CURE took precautions to break links.

"A) What we're doing is taking traditional parts to make a new sum. An interdisciplinary approach to an old situation, the dynamics of conflict.

"B) You're trying to find out why people have conflicts with other people, correct?

"A) In a way, perhaps. You see, man as an animal has conquered the world. Conquered other animals. With ease, as a matter of fact, even though today individual man isn't sure of it. With that out of the way, man has turned to the only challenge left. Conquering other men. The history of war shows that. Well, why should some men conquer and some be conquered? What are the dynamics of that? That's our problem. If you knew, you could defeat any army in the world today with a smaller army. You might say a simple little plan to conquer the world, which I'm sure some politician or militarist would just delight in. But you see the plan is really irrelevant, because conquest is meaningless until you define conqueror and conquered.

"B) You have a plan to conquer the world?

"A) Oh gracious, don't tell me you're one of those. If someone told you he unlocked the atom, would you run out right away to try to use it in a lightbulb or a bomb?

"B) This little plan to conquer the world? Have you achieved it?

"A) What difference does it make? It's only a minor byproduct of our basic work here at XXX.

"B) Would you explain that minor function?

"A) No, not now. Only when we're ready, and then as part of the full corpus of our work. Otherwise, you can imagine the sort of people we'd have running around here, I'd close the forum first."

End of Transcript.

Remo filled the basin with water again and let the transcript go the way of the pictures, first to whiteness, then particles, then dissolve.

That answered one of the why's. A was Nils Brewster, head of the Brewster Forum which had its hands on "a little plan to conquer the world." Brewster would stop everything if he thought the military or the government was moving in. That explained why the forum had been a CURE function. Probably because better than any other group in the world, CURE could watch something or someone without anyone knowing—neither those under surveillance nor those doing the surveillance.

And then the photographs turned up. And that indicated that some other force was involved somehow. Moving in. And the United States could not allow this little plan to conquer the world to go to someone else. And therefore everyone involved, everyone who might know, must die—if it proved necessary.

Remo pulled the plug in the sink and the milky water disappeared. Maybe a sports store in Des Moines, thought Remo, or a bar in Troy, Ohio. That woman in the cab would give him a recommendation. The bar would be nice. Until a customer put a bullet in his head, then took money from the cash register to make it seem like a robbery.

CHAPTER SEVEN

Remo didn't believe it.

He had driven past a sign that read "Brewster Forum," into a lovely little village, then through the village, then past a blank sign which he read in his rear-view mirror as "Brewster Forum."

He turned around on a gravel road and drove the rented car back. Plush little homes, some with sweeping green lawns, others hidden by shrubs, manicured sidewalks and roads, tennis courts, a golf course with only one foursome and a circle of small, quaint cottages.

The August sun blessed the rolling Virginia terrain. A man in blue Bermuda shorts and an old gray shirt pedaled slowly along the asphalt, puffing a pipe rhythmically. He was a small, thin man, with a kind and thoughtful face which Remo recognized in a flash. The man with the giraffe. Remo braked the car.

"Sir," he called out to Dr. Abram Schulter.

The man on the bicycle seemed startled and stopped,

almost capsizing himself. He was the only other person on the street. He looked at Remo, then pointed to himself.

"Me?" asked the foremost neurosurgeon in the world.

"Yes," said Remo, "I'm looking for Brewster Forum."

"Ah, yes. Of course. Why else would you be here? Yes. Natural. Very natural."

"Is this Brewster Forum?

"Yes. Did you miss the signs?"

"No."

"Then what would lead you to believe this is not Brewster Forum?"

"Well, I expected some fences or something."

"Whatever for?"

Remo could not answer that question. What was he to say? Because you're doing something so top secret that you are going to die before your country will let your work go to anyone else?"

Not even a fence. What was probably the highest priority secret project in the nation and not even a fence.

"Well, to keep people out," Remo answered.

"Out of what?," pleasantly asked the son of a bitch who liked to screw toy giraffes.

"Out of this place," said Remo, barely pleasant.

"Why would we want to keep anyone out?"

"I don't know," Remo had to say.

"Then why should we have a fence?"

Remo had to shrug.

"That's an interesting question you asked, son," said Doctor Schulter. "Why does man continuously seek to set boundaries? Is it to keep people out or just to identify who should be kept out?"

In a vein of nastiness which Remo knew he should not allow himself, he snarled, "The latter, of course. It's obvious to anyone who plants tomatoes." And he drove off, leaving the man to puzzle, with the pipe now working furiously in his mouth.

Remo drove back to the cluster of cottages, parking near a fieldstone walk that led to a larger white building with green shutters, shaded by large oaks. The newness of the buildings indicated they had been built for proximity to the towering trees.

Remo followed the fieldstones to the door of the building and knocked. He could see a gravel driveway fifty yards away that led into the circle of cottages but he preferred the walk, a luxury he allowed himself only rarely. Just doing something because he felt like it. Almost like a human being.

The brass knocker was made in a peace symbol design, a circle with the outline of a phantom bomber inside it. At least that was what it had always looked like to the man who was now Remo Pelham, sent to replace Peter McCarthy.

The door opened and down around the doorknob was a little girl with pigtails, round pink cheeks, a smile and dancing eyes.

"Hello," she said. "My name is Stephanie Brewster. I'm six years old and the daughter of Dr. Nils Brewster who is obviously my father since I am his daughter."

"Obviously," said Remo. "I'm Remo Pelham, I'm thirty two years old and I am your new policeman for Brewster Forum. I'm taking the place of the man who went away."

"You mean you're our new security officer. To replace Mr. McCarthy who OD'd last week?"

"OD'd?"

"Yes. He took an overdose of heroin. Would you call that a drug problem? I mean if one man takes an overdose and dies, does that constitute a problem? Obviously, it is no problem for him."

50

Remo looked more closely. Okay, she wasn't a midget. Maybe there was a speaker planted on her.

Stephanie Brewster smiled mischievously. "You're shocked because I've added a new dimension to reality. Six-year-old girls are not supposed to be so aware. But I'm very aware. Prematurely aware, they say, and I'm going to face problems because of it when I grow up unless I learn to adjust my own peer group. That's what daddy says. Only my older sister, Ardath, who is fifteen years old, is just as aware, and she adjusted. So therefore, I should adjust. Right?"

"I guess so," said Remo.

"Would you like to see my daddy?"

"Yes, I would."

"I'll show you where he is if you play Frisbee with me first."

"Why don't you show me where your daddy is now and then we'll play Frisbee?"

"Because if we play Frisbee first, then we'll play Frisbee for sure. But if it's later, then maybe we'll play Frisbee. Reality is so much more meaningful than a promise, don't you think? Especially a promise from someone over eight."

"I never trusted anyone over eight myself," Remo said. When you are overwhelmed, you are overwhelmed.

"Do you have a Frisbee?"

"No, I'm afraid I don't."

"But you said you would play Frisbee with me and if you don't have a Frisbee, how can we play Frisbee together?" Her faint brows furrowed and her mouth turned down. Her blue eyes filled with tears. She stamped a foot. "You said you'd play Frisbee with me and you're not playing Frisbee. You said you'd play and you don't have a Frisbee. And how can we play Frisbee if you don't have one? I don't have a Frisbee."

Then Stephanie Brewster covered her eyes and cried like the six-year-old girl she was. And Remo picked her up and held her and promised her a Frisbee, but she would have to stop rubbing her eyes because that was bad for them.

"I know," sobbed Stephanie Brewster. "The retina is sensitive to pressure."

"Would you like to learn a Korean proverb?"

"What?" asked Stephanie cautiously, clinging to her unhappiness lest the offering fail to match in value the tears she was shedding.

"You should rub your eyes only with your elbows."

"But you can't rub your eyes with your elbows."

Remo smiled. And Stephanie laughed. "I see. I see. You're not supposed to rub your eyes."

"That's right."

"I like you. Come, take me into the office."

Remo walked into an office off the living room. And he was horrified to learn that this was where Nils Brewster did most of his work, that the papers scattered about were the thinking of Brewster Forum, and no doubt contained that little plan for world conquest. No gates, no locks, and a six-year-old girl who said,

"I don't understand that yet, but you can read it. But leave the papers in the same order. Daddy's fussy."

Leave them in the same order. Her father might die for those papers because he was fussy and left them in the same order. Remo felt sick.

But he forced himself to think of millions of people and their lives. He stretched thousands out on roads, smiling, holding hands, every home in America, every family, every crowd. And he knew that if the word came, he would do his duty and kill—even if it was the glorious, brilliant Nils Brewster, and even though his death would shatter this delicious child, Stephanie.

It was Remo's good fortune that he soon met Nils Brewster, and the meeting made his possible assignment a great deal easier.

CHAPTER EIGHT

Nils Brewster was not dressed in chains as he had been for his nude portrait. He wore a short-sleeved blue shirt, chinos and sneakers. His hair flew about his head like tornado-whipped tumbleweed.

Stephanie had gone off to tell her mother about the new director of security, and had left Remo in the only large building in the compound that might have housed a laboratory. It did not. It was an auditorium, now filled with people crowded around tables.

The first thing Doctor Brewster said to Remo was: "Shhhhh."

"I'm Remo Pelham, the new. . . ."

"I know, I know. Shhhhhh.'"

He turned and Remo followed. It was a chess tournament. Remo would learn later that Brewster Forum had not only a chess tournament, but a chess instructor, a tennis pro, a golf pro, a singing teacher, a karate instructor, a musical conductor, its own little newspaper—published for the twenty-three people who could understand what was going on in the forum, including to Remo's awesome shock, a Russian—and a sky-diving coach.

"We provide what people need or ask for," Brewster told him later.

"No skiing?"

"The weather's not right here. We send our people who want to learn to the Big Boulder Ski School at Lake Harmony. They teach *natur teknik*, the best method of learning. You learn parallel right away."

"That's nice," Remo would say, wondering for just a moment if Nils Brewster had not devised the most beautiful hustle of the Twentieth Century.

But that afternoon, it was chess. A pudgy man with bulging brown eyes and flicking wrists was in an endgame with a hulk of a whitehaired man who hovered over the board like a weightlifter preparing himself for a record hoist. The pudge was Dr. James Ratchett, the homosexual in the cape, versus the Jesuit of the missionary position.

Ratchett spied Remo and pointed a delicate finger. "Who is that?" he asked. It was an obvious ploy to divert Father Boyle's attention away from the board because, on the two buttoned clock, it was Father Boyle's time running out.

"The new security director," whispered Brewster.

"Our new flatfoot," taunted Ratchett.

"Shhhhh," said Brewster to Remo before Remo said anything.

"Are you Irish like our deceased Mister McCarthy?"

Remo said nothing. He just stared at the board.

Remo had been taught chess and did not like it. He had been taught chess, not for the intricacy of the moves nor for the concentration it required. He was taught chess simply to realize that each move changed the board. It was something people tended to forget in life; that every move altered things in some way and that preconceived operations needed flexibility to be worthwhile. Basically, chess taught Remo how to look. He looked now around the room and saw the karate lover, in clothes this time, watching closely. Another interested observer was a man in a dark suit and dark tie, who Remo found out later was the chess instructor.

"I asked you a question, cop," said Ratchett. "Are you Irish like our deceased Mister McCarthy?"

"Shhhhh," said Brewster angrily to Remo who was silent.

"When I speak to you, you will answer me," said Ratchett, huffing himself in his chair. "Answer me."

"I don't think I'm Irish," Remo said. It was a bland tone, one used for getting rid of annoying questions and questioners.

"You don't think you're Irish. You don't think. Don't you know? After all, I thought all Irishmen knew they were Irish. Otherwise, why would the little dears all become policemen and priests? I'm playing against a priest, now, you know."

Father Boyle did not look up, but moved his rook from an inactive corner to the center of the board. Ordinarily, it would not be a bad move. But now it was a bad move because Ratchett had more men attacking the square than the priest had defending. Under those circumstances, the priest would succumb.

Ratchett was suddenly quiet and on the board with all his attention. Father Boyle looked over his shoulder and extended his hand to Remo. "Hi, I'm Bob Boyle. We're all a little bit nuts here. I think it's a function of intelligence."

"I'm Remo Pelham," said Remo, taking the hand. Well, pleasant or not, the priest would go with the rest if the word came down. Remo wasn't a judge, just an operative.

"Shhhh," said Nils Brewster.

"Get off it, Nils," said the priest.

"He's not to disturb anyone," Brewster snapped back. "I don't really like his presence here in the first place. If we didn't need federal funding, I wouldn't allow him on the premises. You know how they are, the whole fascistic mentality."

"You're the biggest fascist I've ever met, Nils. And also the worst snob. Now get off it."

Ratchett, red faced, snapped a piece angrily down on the board, putting more pressure on the imperilled square.

"What is going on here,?" he screamed. "Why must I suffer these indignities from a cop? Everytime I move, someone's yelling. Yelling. Yelling," Ratchett's voice rose like a happy hawk. His hands twittered violently. His fat face flushed.

"You Irish bastards are in league to defeat me. That's why you're here. It's a plot—that's all you Irish are good for. Why don't you stop skulking around trying to upset me and act like a man? Tell Boyle how to move. Go ahead. Go ahead. Make your perfidy complete. Go ahead.

"Look everyone. A cop is going to help Father Boyle play chess. A cop who plays chess." Ratchett laughed out a haughty condemnation and looked around for approval. Finding none in the onlooking faces, he increased his vehemence.

"I demand you tell Father Boyle how to win. He can use your help. Anyone who believes in God can use all the help he can get. Go ahead. Right now. No protest. There are two possible ways he can win. I am assuming you know chess. Father Boyle does not. Tell him how."

It was the three months of peak that got to Remo, the

three months of staying where he should not have stayed mentally or physically. That and Brewster Forum and these lunatics and being told that he must arrange for the deaths of these harmless twits, just because their brilliance might lead them to a wrong corridor.

So Remo made a mistake. Even before he knew what he was doing, he said:

"There are three ways Father Boyle can beat you. The first two require an error on your part. But the third he can do alone. His knight to your Rook 3, uncovering check by the queen. It's a smothered mate in three."

Remo had spoken softly, almost like the tender point of a sermon. At first Ratchett was going to laugh, then his face became blank. It was obvious he had not seen the move. And as the move became apparent to others in the audience there were little sounds. And Father Boyle began to laugh, a full hearty laugh, and others laughed with him, and Ratchett became white. White hot. If man could become hate, Dr. James Ratchett was hate.

Remo did not laugh, because he knew he should be spanked. Lectures were for grownups and beatings were for men. But spankings were for little boys who took up prideful challenges that could so easily get them killed. Stupid. Stupid, Remo thought. You entered as a dumb cop and lest anyone spot you as a real danger by some accident, you went out of your way to let them know that maybe you weren't so dumb. A cop, all right, but a cop to be watched. The greenest rookie wouldn't do something that stupid. Give away surprise and you give away your life. How the lecture had been drilled into him, and how logical it was:

"You must isolate what you wish to do. Most personal assaults fail because they attempt to do too much, not the

58

least of which is to gain respect from your target." Those were the words of Chiun, the instructor.

"That's stupid," Remo had answered. "No one would do that."

"Most people do," said Chiun quietly. "They show off for their victim. This is because they wish not so much to harm the other person as to force the other to recognize their superiority. You see it even among prize fighters. How foolish.

"If you learn no other lesson, learn this one, and it will do more to keep you alive than any other. The most dangerous man is the man who does not appear dangerous. Say it after me."

"Okay," said Remo, imitating the squeaky sing-song of the aged Korean. "The most dangerous man is the man who does not appear dangerous. Say it after me."

"Ooooh," said Chiun, clutching his chest. "Ooooh." And Remo had jumped to his feet from the little cushions they sat on and moved to steady the elderly man.

"Set me down, please. Please. On my back." Chiun groaned again and Remo carefully placed his hands under Chiun's arms and slowly placed the white frosted head on a pillow.

"I do not look dangerous now," said Chiun, in obvious pain.

"No, you do not," Remo said tenderly.

"Good," said Chiun, driving a finger into the back of Remo's rib cage, rendering him a helpless cripple on the floor. It had felt like pliers tearing his lower rib from his spinal column, causing such pain that Remo was unable to cry out or even to groan.

When the eternity of the moment was over and Remo could scream, then breathe, and then lie quivering, Chiun had said: "I cause you this pain so that you should remem-

59

ber. Never be dangerous in the eyes of men whom you plan to combat. Never. I cause you pain because I love you. Yes. Love. True love is doing what is good for a person. False love is doing only that which causes that person to love you. The love I have for you is shown in this pain that I give you. The pain is your lesson, best learned."

When Remo could speak, but not yet get up, he said:

"You yellow dink bastard shit. Stop the pain."

"I love you too much to stop the pain."

"You no good scumbag. Stop the pain."

"No, my son."

Then Remo went for his emotional lungs. "You look like a Chinaman." He knew Chiun hated the Chinese almost as much as he hated the people in the next village.

"You shall not tempt me to rob you of your lesson. I have given too much to you to be robbed of the gift. You see, never again can I pretend this weakness and catch you off guard. I have, in a small way, given you a piece of my future, a piece of my life. I have given to you the knowledge that I am dangerous."

"I always knew you were dangerous, you little yellow China bastard."

"Ah, but not in that way."

"Okay, okay. I'm sorry. I've learned. Stop the pain, please."

"True love does not allow it."

"Hate me then," said Remo. "For heaven's sake, hate me and stop the fucking pain."

"No. A gift is a gift."

"Your generosity will kill me, you creepy, fish-eating fuck. When does the pain stop?"

"All your days you may have it. It is a lifelong gift. Ribs can be like that."

The pain lessened, but continued from day to day, and from day to day, Remo begged Chiun to do what he must to stop it. Every night, he would interrupt Chiun's sleep to tell him. And in the second week, Chiun who could endure almost anything but the loss of sleep, succumbed.

Remo had nudged him in the very dark predawn. "It still hurts me, you bastard."

And wearily, Chiun sat up from his mat, and told Remo: "I am sorry, my son. But I do not love you this much. I must sleep." And he pressed his fingers on the base of Remo's spine, working his way to the rib of pain and then with a slap at the pain, the pain was gone and Remo felt exquisite relief that almost brought tears to his eyes.

"Thank you. Thank you," he said.

And Chiun had said: "I am sorry, my son. I am sorry I had to do that. But I would not live much longer without my sleep. I am an old man. And I only love you with a part of my life. Not all of it." He lay down on his mat and before he passed back into slumber, he said, "Forgive me."

And Remo had forgiven with a laugh. But standing now over the chess board, he would not forgive himself. And he realized that he had been unworthy of the gift that Chiun had given him. Stupid. Stupid. Stupid, Remo thought. You stupid, idiotic bastard. You entered this room a zero, and now you're part of the goddam dynamics of the place, with friends and enemies, and it's just going to be that much tougher to perform if the order comes to waste them.

CHAPTER NINE

The man once known as Dr. Hans Frichtmann had seen the move. Nothing new. Nothing innovative. Rather standard. Nothing that couldn't be learned. Yet, for its purpose and in context, brilliant. They hadn't sent a McCarthy this time. Did they suspect that McCarthy was not the victim of an accidental overdose, that he was murdered?

This was the real thing this time. Could they know about him and his daughter? Perhaps, but doubtful. More likely, they knew about McCarthy as a murder victim. Yet, where were the legions of men in shined shoes and clean shirts and schoolboy honest complexions? There would certainly be all that for a full crackdown.

Well, perhaps not. Maybe this Remo Pelham person was the best they had. It was strange that he had somehow evaded the men who met him on the ferryboat. Dr. Hans Frichtmann would have to deal with him. The sooner the better.

He waited until everyone had left the hall, then went to

Ratchett's home. Ratchett had been the first to leave, huffing out indignantly.

He walked awhile with his daughter, up the tree-graced lane and over the sweetly-whistling brook to Ratchett's house, that white plastered obscenity shaped like an egg, that new design that only an American could call art. Only an American or a Frenchman. How wise it had been on everyone's part to put it behind a knoll, invisible to sensitive eyes.

"He would make a fantastic lay," said the daughter.

"My dear, for you anything is a fantastic lay," he said wearily.

"Not anything."

"What is excluded? Please let me know. I will buy one."

"I wouldn't screw a black."

"A black man, that is? A black dog or black horse is different?"

"It's not the same."

"No, it is not the same. What makes you this way?"

"Watching people herded into ovens and having one's home lit with lampshades of human skin might be conducive to some deviation in a little girl."

"Yes. That. Well, it was the times."

"And I have my times, father."

"Yes, I suppose you do."

"I want that man. I must have him."

"Not yet."

"It's always not yet. Every day is not yet. Yesterday was not yet. Tomorrow will be not yet. I am tired of being deprived. Always deprived. Changing names, changing homes. All the time. Running. From Americans and British and French and Russians. Now even from our own people in Germany and God help us, from the Jews. It disgusts me to run from Jews. I want to tell the whole world who we are, what we are. We should be proud. We are Nazis."

"Quiet."

"Nazis. Nazis. Nazis. *Seig heil.*"

"Quiet."

"Do I get him?"

"Yes. But not yet."

"Nazi, Nazi, Nazi. Dr. Hans Frichtmann, of Treblinka, Buchenwald and various other resorts of final solution. Dr. Hans. . . ."

"All right. All right. You can have him."

"When?"

"Soon."

"With the pictures too?"

"I don't know."

"I like being a star, daddy. I like to see your face when you photograph me. That is the best part."

"All right. Go home now, dear. I must see Dr. Ratchett," he said wearily.

"I will go. It makes you sick to see me do those things?"

"Yes."

"That is the best part."

He watched his daughter stride happily away, putting another victory in her pocket, then entered the home of Dr. James Ratchett. Ratchett had not yet entered his special place, but was cutting at a dark wedge which looked like dried chewing tobacco, but was really hashish. The wedge was the size of a domino and he watched Ratchett's pudgy fingers work the razor at an edge, cutting slivers into the small bronze bowl of a pipe. Every other sliver missed.

"The beast," Ratchett said, "I can't even fill my pipe."

"Poor man. How could they let this happen to you? Here, I will prepare your pipe." They sat in Ratchett's living room, a dramatic affair of black and white. Behind the fireplace, bordered by two curved elephant tusks, was the place he knew Ratchett would enter.

The back of the fireplace was the lone slit of dark red. The white tusks surrounded it and were surrounded themselves by a circle of black. Ratchett was the only person at Brewster Forum who did not grasp the symbolism of his design. But then a man's sickness is invariably hidden from his soul.

"That policeman made a very good move," he said, packing the pipe for Ratchett.

"If I knew that cop knew what he knew, I never would have played that way against Boyle. You know I'm a better player than that."

"I know."

"It won't count in the tournament, will it?"

"I'm afraid it must."

"It shouldn't. Boyle had help."

"You offered to allow it."

"That Boyle. I could beat him any day of the week. Any day."

"Yes, you can."

"I could kill him."

"What for?"

"For doing that to me."

"He didn't do anything to you."

"He took that cop's advice, that night watchman who is all of a sudden allowed to play in our tournaments."

"Yes, he took the advice. But who gave it? Did you see him laugh at you?"

"He didn't laugh."

"He smirked and started the laughing. All the time he

65

knew you were only toying with Boyle and he knew you could beat him in a fair game. But he saw he could beat you, the only way he could, by taking your generosity toward Boyle and turning it on you."

"Yes. The only way he could beat me. Humiliate me."

"Of course, and everybody laughed along with him."

"The bastards."

"They can't help it. As long as that man is here, they will laugh at you."

"Nonsense. They know he's only a policeman."

"They will laugh the more."

"No."

"Yes. When they see you. They will laugh inside."

"You're a beast for telling me this."

"I am your friend. A friend tells the truth."

"You're still a beast."

He handed Ratchett the pipe and answered: "Perhaps I should not have told you. After all, there is only one way you can humiliate him and you would not stoop to that."

"What way?"

"Your friends on the motorcycles. Your, what do you call them, rough trade. Imagine a policeman who cannot stop hoodlums."

"You're right. I wouldn't do that. Nils would be in a snit. An absolute snit."

"How would he know it's you?"

"I would never stoop that low. Never." Dr. James Ratchett smiled. "I'm in the right mood now. Would you like to join me in my place? Share the peace pipe?"

"Thank you no, I must get home."

"Besides," said Doctor Ratchett, "even if Nils did find out, how could he replace Dr. James Ratchett?"

"How could he, indeed?"

"Of course, I would never stoop so low."

"Of course."

"Be at the offices tomorrow at noon," Ratchett said with a giggle, and ducked between the elephant tusks into the next room.

The man once known as Dr. Hans Frichtmann smiled at Ratchett's back, then left the egg-shaped house. He would see what he would see. Some chess moves, he knew very well, could be very destructive. Especially the ones that appeared brilliant at first.

This Remo Pelham person had made a serious mistake. With luck, it would be a fatal mistake. And by the time they sent yet another to replace him, the people who had drafted the plan to conquer the world would be in the control of another power, who would know how to use that plan. And Dr. Hans Frichtmann would be gone.

CHAPTER TEN

Nils Brewster would have to get it over with. He didn't let garbage collect in the kitchen. Paid his bills on time. Saw the dentist when his teeth acted up. There was no reason to put it off any longer. He would do it. Get it over with.

"Send in Remo what's-his-name," said Nils Brewster into his intercom and promptly felt quite satisfied with his integrity.

His office faced out onto a circle, a mass of green ringed by black gravel. Rimming the circle were the white cottages of the forum, which served as both offices and living quarters for the forum's top brass. Farther back, beyond the ring of cottages, one could see more traditional lab and office buildings where the hirelings worked. The view of the circle was piece-mealed through small, cozy, wood-encased windows in Brewster's office, which made the world look like a chess game. The trees were mid-board and the sky was enemy territory.

A white couch graced the far wall of Brewster's office,

and original paintings, mostly geometric forms in day-glo colors, hung from the walls. On the floor was a Polar Bear Rug, "a little whimsey of mine, Lord knows I get so few indulgences." That little indulgence had cost more than $12,000. It was paid for by one of the funding foundations which annually produced a report showing how it made life better for mankind, particularly black mankind. For some reason, the $12,000 was linked to understanding black rage.

The office was pleasant and warm. That was the way Nils Brewster had intended it to be, a setting mirroring the warmth and wisdom and understanding of the tweed draped hulk who occupied it.

When Remo entered, he saw the hulk. He saw it puffing away at a pipe, engrossed in being Nils Brewster, Ph.D, Chicago U., director of Brewster Forum, author of several books which a few thousand owned, a few hundred read, and seven or eight understood. He saw the hulk was about to tolerate him.

"Glad to see you," Doctor Brewster crooned in a low Massachusetts mumble which crackled saliva on the S's. "You're Remo . . . Remo. . . ."

"Remo Pelham."

"That's right. Our chess-playing policeman. Well, what can I do for you?"

"Well, first of all, I'd like to know what you do here?"

"Why?"

"Because I can't figure out what I'm supposed to do here, until I find out what you do here, can I?"

"Never mind."

"Never mind?"

Remo stood before the desk still, waiting to be offered a seat. The offer did not come, so he sat anyway.

"That's right, never mind." Brewster said this with a smile.

"Why should I never mind?"

"Simply because you wouldn't understand."

"Try me."

"I'd rather not."

"I'd rather you would," Remo said.

"Really now," Brewster said, crossing a leg while sucking the fumes from the lit pipe. "You'd rather I would. Well, do you know that the only reason you're here is because of a government grant? You come with it. Now I don't wish to make your stay here unpleasant, but you are an unwanted guest. Already, last night, with your uncivilized behavior at the chess tournament, you have created dissension among my staff. I can do without that. I can also do without your skulking about trying to provide security and protection for things that need neither security nor protection."

"Did McCarthy understand that?"

"McCarthy was a policeman, for heaven's sakes."

"Who is a dead policeman."

"Right. A dead policeman." Brewster said it as if he had been asked to say a prayer for a departed piece of roast beef. "Oppressive violence—that is, violence in reaction to violence—breeds greater violence. A pure example is McCarthy. Do you understand what I'm talking about?"

"I think you're trying to say that McCarthy got himself killed."

"Right. You're brighter than I thought. Now, let's take this supposition a little farther. Let us assume that violence is an expurgative, that it is—try to follow me—a natural and necessary occurrence and that to try to curb it or redirect it produces awesomely more-devastating circumstances, by a basic geometric progression of intensity, an intensity that we cannot now measure but that we will ultimately use as a guideline, much in the way of E equals MC square. Do you follow?"

"Yes. You're full of shit."

"Really? How?"

"Never mind. I really don't think I can explain it to you."

Brewster broke into the kind of delighted grin a father gets when his six year old son challenges him to checkers.

"You can't explain it to me?"

"No. No, I can't," Remo said, and he was not smiling or enjoying what he said. "I can only say that violence has all the virtue of a cut into flesh. Done to cure—to heal—it is good. Done to harm, it is bad. The act itself is neither good nor bad. Just painful."

"But don't you see, Mr. Pelham, that for violence to be employed for good or bad is impossible. There is no good or bad." Doctor Brewster sat with limbs close to body and smiled as if he had a belly full of warm milk.

"You are full of shit," Remo said.

"And you are another fascist functionary who dribbles righteousness until I cross your palm with silver. The good guys and the bad guys. Law and order versus the people in black hats. It is not that way, Mr. Pelham."

"It can be no other way, Doctor Brewster," Remo said and he caught his jaw trembling. Goddam it, it was the peak. More than three months of it this and he was coming apart at the seams. Sitting here, trying to talk sense to this liberalistic lunatic. Brewster was still talking:

"Please. We really just cannot afford this here, of all places. I am willing to discuss anything you wish, but please no overreaction. You have a job to do, such as it is, and I have a job to do. We're here together, let's make the most of it."

71

"What makes you think McCarthy was killed?" Remo said, calm again.

"I knew you would come back to that. I think he was killed because he is not the sort of man to use heroin. To use heroin, you must have a basic dissatisfaction with your role in life. McCarthy never had enough imagination to be dissatisfied. He was a bear-in-a-saloon type, Knights of Columbus, worry about mortgage. Very nice fellow, indeed. And frankly, I prefer him to you. McCarthy was a realist."

"And knowing or believing he was murdered, you didn't give your suspicions to anyone?"

"And have this place crawling with law enforcement types?"

Brewster sucked on his pipe with finality, a man who saw the world in clear light while the rest muddled in the fog. The Remo Pelhams of the world who comprehended nothing, even of such an elemental subject as violence.

Through the English glass windows of the office came a distant roar that rather rapidly became louder, than a symphony of belching exhausts that rode into the circle, and then round and round the small blue fountain.

The motorcycle riders looked like refugees from the SS. They had black leather jackets, high peaked caps, and swastikas on their backs. Unlike the SS, however, they were unshaven, and there was no uniformity to their cycles, green and red and yellow and black, festooned with ribbons, banners and skull, leather pieces flowing over highly polished chrome.

Brewster went to the window. Remo behind him. Out of the cottages, the office-homes that surrounded the circle, came the department directors of Brewster Forum. There was Father Boyle and Professor Schulter. There was Ferrante, and on the right was Ratchett. And there was a fifth. She came from the farthest cottage. A young woman who could have been twenty or thirty. Her high cheek bones and strong aristocratic nose were ageless. Her dark hair flowed down over her shoulders like a royal mantle. Her lips were etched deeply in milk smooth skin.

While her colleagues hovered by their doors, she went to the edge of the gravel. The leader of the motorcycles aimed at her and charged her headlong, swerving sharply at the last moment.

She smiled. Remo thought, she's amused.

Another cyclist circled behind her and still she did not move. The pack roared around again, and this time the leader drove into a skid stop that sprayed gravel at her feet. Still smiling, she turned and walked back calmly to her office.

Remo smiled to himself. She was a rare one. If she had tried to run, the group would have been at her like a pack of dogs. But she waited until the leader temporarily turned off the aggression by sliding into that skid stop and then she just walked away. She disappeared as an attack object. Quite a performance.

Now Ratchett waddled out to the leader so rapidly he appeared to be skipping. His hair flowed behind him and his tiny fingers tickled the air excitedly at the farthest reaches of his arms. He whispered into the gold-ringed ear of the leader who grabbed the collar of Ratchett's velveteen shirt and began to twist, as Ratchett's face grew pink, then red. When Ratchett managed to get a roll of bills out of his pocket, the hand loosened. Ratchett kissed the wrist of the hand at his throat; then the leader released him and he stood like a little boy hiding his privates in a public shower.

The leader strode the sidewalk, his boots galonking on

73

the pavement, his followers' boots adding support to the galonk, galonk, galonk toward Brewster's office.

Brewster turned to Remo. "Now I don't want any trouble. Remember violence begets worse, etc. We can just ignore the whole thing."

Remo went back to his chair.

"Hey cop," yelled the leader of the gang. "Come out here."

Remo stage-whispered to Brewster: "I'm doing nothing, sitting right here."

"Good."

"Hey, Pelham. You straight shit. Get out here." The leader was over six-feet-six and massive. But the bulk was weight-lifter's bulk. His walk was a pose. His challenge was a pose. Mr. Six-Foot-Six had won most of his battles by posing menacingly. His major weapon was fear in the hearts of the timid.

Now he nodded and a follower threw an object—yes, it was a rock, judged Remo, just before it crashed through the window and broke into the natural rhythm of Brewster's nose. Brewster spun and gasped and shrieked and covered his nose. Then he looked at his hands. They were dressed in blood, flowing down his wrists into his tweed jacket.

"Oh, no. The bastards. My nose."

Indeed, the nose was broken, a rapidly-spreading red glob that released large amounts of blood. Broken it was, tragic it wasn't.

"It's broken, that's all," said Remo. "Keep your hands away from it. Only the splinter can be dangerous."

"Oh, no. The pain. The blood. You're security officer. Do something. I order it. I even give permission. Do something. Call the police. Call a doctor."

"Call the oppressive, trouble-creating counterforce?"

74

"Don't be so smartass, Pelham. I'm bleeding. Go out there and thrash the scum. If you have a gun, use it. Kill the little bastards."

Remo walked to the window. The seven-man gang was growing restive. Their next step would be to walk into Brewster's office, and that might wind up causing damage to Brewster's files and the work of the forum. Remo would have to go out and work in front of witnesses.

"Excuse me," he told Brewster. "I'll only be a moment."

He pushed open the door to the courtyard, and stood there a minute telling himself, no matter how many months he had been at peak, he'd better not slip and kill one of these lugs.

The head lug took Remo's momentary hesitation for fear.

"Come over here, you fag bastard," he called.

Remo walked up to him, gauging the distance, exactly three and one half feet away, the precise distance for the toe kick to the kneecap.

"Did you call me, sir?" he said to Six-Foot-Six as the other half-dozen cyclists lined up behind their leader. From left to right in the row, they were carrying chains, lug wrench, knife, chain, chain and knife.

The leader posed. He brandished his size and weight.

Ratchett was far down the courtyard, masturbating by rubbing his hands inside his pants pockets. None of his colleagues noticed, their eyes were on Remo.

"Yeah, I called you, fag. What do you think of that?"

"What do I think of what, sir?" Remo drew his right hand closer to his side, and slightly turned it palm facing front. The fingernails would be good for two eyeballs when the second row made its move.

"You're a fag. And you like to cheat people at games."

"Very true, sir," Remo said. He bent his left elbow slightly. He must be sure the elbow would hit the nose; an inch too low and the blow could be fatal.

"You like to cause trouble."

"Very true, sir," Remo said. He extended the fingers on his left hand, then pulled his thumb back against the palm, almost like cocking a revolver.

Mister Six-Foot-Six was becoming confused. "You're a fag," he insisted.

"Well, sir," Remo said. "I've really enjoyed our conversation, but I must be about my business. Unless there's something else you'd like to ask me."

"You're a faggot. A fairy. A queer. Do you like being that?" Six-Foot-Six was getting desperate now. Time to end the nonsense.

"No, I don't like being that," Remo said. "You know what I like?"

"What?"

"I like being called names by shitfaces like you. Because it justifies all the painful things I'm going to do to you. And these turds that hover around you, like flies around a pig's ass."

Ratchett clutched in awesome excitement at his organ.

"I don't want to have to look at your ugly pimpled face anymore or hear that belching that you call words. Now step forward, shit. Step forward one inch, and I'm going to fix you so that you'll never walk again without the pain reminding you of me. Come on. Just one inch."

The leader laughed. But his followers didn't. They waited, and their silence shouted at him, and accused him, and finally, in frustration, he stepped forward, just one inch, and then he moved himself into something very fast that seemed to plunge a knife into his kneecap, and then there was a wrench, and then the sky, and then that awful tearing, and he was staring at the sky and it became dark, then black, then nothing.

Remo worked the others rather lightly. The right hand fingernails took care of an eyeball each on chain and knife at the right end of the line.

The elbow took care of chain at the left, and Remo was pleased when it neatly smashed the nose like a dried cracker, without slipping off toward the potentially-fatal upper lip. The edge of his left hand cracked like a baseball bat against the forehead of lug wrench, second from the left, and he dropped in a heap.

This wouldn't do. Five of them were down, and Remo still hadn't moved from the spot. All that was left was knife and chain in the middle.

If Remo had raised his arms and shouted "boo," they would have fun. But Remo needed them. He didn't want it to look too easy. He backed up a step, encouraging knife and chain to charge. He moved around between the two of them, lunging, blocking, making it all look very hard, and then suddenly he didn't give a shit who was watching, and he busted an ear drum on each one of them.

So there they were, seven of them groaning on the gravel. Ratchett spent, Brewster, who had come to the door, on the verge of a scream of gratitude, and Remo holding his head. Remo was holding his head because he had collected some blood from one of the seven and he put it on his head to show a wound. Then, still bent over, he forced his mind onto his blood vessels—out, in, circulation—very strong thoughts of fire, oppression, sweltering sun taking his fluids, and was finally able to work up a sweat.

"I love you. I love you," yelled Ratchett. Then he ran inside, presumably, Remo thought, to change his pants.

"That ode's still bovid," Brewster called through his broken nose. "Kick hib or sobthid."

"You kick him," Remo said.

"I deed a doctor," Brewster said and vanished indoors.

With the exception of their leader whose knee cap had turned suddenly to jelly, the cyclists were capable of driving away. They carried Mr. Six-Foot-Six.

Then something very surprising happened. The staff of Brewster Forum—the faces in the pictures, the new intellectuals—crowded around Remo like school children, congratulating him. There was Ferrante. And Schulter. There was even the forum's chess instructor, who said something about "a game some time."

But Remo wasn't paying attention. He was looking for one who wasn't there, the black-haired beauty who had vanished into the last cottage as soon as the fight ended.

CHAPTER ELEVEN

It was noon, and as he did every day, Remo checked Dial-a-Prayer in Chicago. The Reverend Sminstershoop was still in Psalms.

Genesis would have begun a get-ready countdown. Ecclesiastes would have given Remo a day to finish his assignment. Deuteronomy meant all plans out the window, wipe out the place and split.

But Psalms just meant another day at peak readiness. Yea, though he walked through the valley of death, he could not relax, let the tension drain, recoup his powers. He feared only the evil of diminishing every day. Already, if he were to risk the cat fall, he knew he would not just make a sound, he would probably get a concussion.

So he spoke a number into the tape recording. The number was of his telephone booth with the area code placed last, the traditional way of destroying as many links as possible, even if those links were to your own people, monitoring incoming phone calls for people they did not know.

And he hung up, not by returning the receiver, but by leaning his phone arm down on the cradle. He kept it there five minutes while chattering away to no one. On the first buzz before the bell engaged in the first ring, Remo released the cradle.

"It's me," he said, that being enough identification. At one time he had a number, but he could never remember it, and Smith finally told him to forget it. "Look, I spoke with everyone but the woman here. And I don't believe the pictures. Were the photos possibly phonys?"

"No. We got the original negatives. We matched the grains right from the beginning. Why do you ask?"

"I just wanted to be helpful."

"Don't be helpful. The photos aren't your primary purpose there. Have you arranged for . . . for whatever might be necessary?" Even on a scrambled phone that could not be tapped, Smith was cautious.

"That's all done," Remo said. "This is a togetherness joint. Every night, all the boys gather around the recreation room. Give me five minutes and I can rig the air-conditioning to do the job."

"How about individuals?"

"No problem there, either. I can talk them all to death."

"Is that supposed to be funny? What the hell is the matter with you. You're getting . . . unstable."

Remo knew that was the second worst word in Smith's vocabulary. Worst was "incompetent."

"I want to go off peak."

"No."

"Why not?"

"Because you're on a job."

"I'm losing my edge."

"Don't give me that gymnasium talk. Edge this, peak that. Just stay in shape."

"I'm slipping."

"You'll do."

"I'm going slowly crazy."

"You always were."

"I think I'm getting incompetent."

"Would one day help?"

"Yes."

"One day might be all right. Yes. Take it if you need it. But don't make it a big day. We don't know what the sister agencies might come up with, and when you might have to move."

"Okay." Remo changed the subject before Smith had a chance to change his mind. "Did you get the package I sent you? The wallets?"

"Yes. We're working on them, but they're difficult to trace. By the way. . . ."

"No more 'by the ways'."

"By the way," Smith persisted. "Have you found out what they do there? I mean . . . their little plan?"

"You wouldn't understand it if I told you," Remo said, hanging up. He was already halfway toward becoming an intellectual, the main ingredient being to have someone around to be a non-intellectual.

Maybe that's what the forum was all about. An elaborate hustle. Remo didn't believe that any of the scientists at Brewster Forum, up to and including its founder, could have produced a plan to conquer a phone booth. Not one of the scientists had given even a hint of doing any kind of work the government might possibly think was important. And Remo had talked to all of them, except for the dark-haired beauty, Dr. Deborah Hirshbloom.

Strangely enough, he already liked them. Very smart,

Remo. Now all you have to do is to fall in love with Dr. Deborah Hirshbloom. That would really be smart.

Perhaps if he had been trained to work up a hate. Professional football players do it. Why not him? Because, sweetheart, you were taught to work up a nothing. Start hating and that's the next best thing to loving for making you incompetent. Shit, next thing you know, you'll be a human being. And then look where all that wonderful money would go. Down the drain. All that money that was spent to make you the wonderful nothing you are. A man who can hold his arm extended, absolutely motionless, not one shake, for fifty-three minutes. Let's hear it for the geniuses who run this country. Let's hear it for CURE. Hush. Hush. Hush.

Staying at peak does wonders for the mental processes. Yes, Remo, talk to yourself. Let's hear it for CURE. Hush. Hush. Hush.

You've heard of the right hand not knowing what the left is doing. Well, our cuticles don't know what our knuckles are doing. Let's hear it for CURE. Hush. Hush. Hush.

Okay, pal, slow down. That lady in the car saw you laughing to yourself. Slow it down. Move the oxygen around. Go back to that room they gave you during training. You remember the room. The quiet room. Remember every detail, just how it felt. Quiet room. Black carpeting. The couch.

"You can always come back to this room in your mind," Chiun had said. "This is your safety, your retreat. When your mind or your body needs rest, come back. You are safe here. And loved here. No one may enter whom you do not invite. Just send your mind back here."

And Remo went back to the room and just sat with Chiun as he had sat before. And his mind cooled and some strength returned. The woman's face was familiar. Or was it? People are recognized more by the way they walk or hold their head than by features. Features are only the final, the last, proof of recognition.

It was a hard face, a very old thirty five, under smooth flaxen hair. She rested a bare arm on the window opening of the convertible.

"Hi there, fella. How are you?"

"Do I know you?"

"No, but I know you. The chess game. You couldn't see me. Magnificent move."

"Oh," said Remo.

"I'm Anna Stohrs. Dr. Stohrs' daughter, the chess instructor. I'm also president of the daughters' association of Brewster Forum."

"A lot of daughters here?"

"Yes, but none like me."

"That's nice," Remo said.

"I think you're cute. Let's."

"Let's what?"

"You know."

"No."

"Why not?"

"I'm a virgin."

"I don't believe you."

"Okay, I'm not a virgin," Remo agreed.

He could see her play her eyes down his body, lingering at his groin.

"Would you do it for pay?" she asked.

"No."

"Why not?"

"You think you're cute, don't you?"

She smiled an even-toothed smile, an attractive but

hard smile. She tilted her head back in arrogance. "I know I'm cute, copper."

She had switched tactics, to pricking the ego, setting herself as a tough prize, much like the heroine of a lovely little novel Remo had once read. He leaned into the car.

"Not caring about someone," he said, "is apologizing. I apologize. I have an appointment."

And he left for the circle of the Forum, to attempt to track down Doctor Hirshbloom, to finish the set-up on her before he took his wonderful day off.

Strange about her. All the other scientists had sought him out after the incident with the cycle gang. Father Boyle had been the first interview and a surprisingly difficult fix. Like most Jesuits, he made a career of not seeming like a priest, while deeply acting out his faith.

He sat with his big feet on his very little desk. Remo had learned to distrust people who sat with their feet on the desk. It was usually a come-on by ho, ho, ho, one-big-happy-family fakers trying to get a hustler's edge.

But Remo was willing to forgive and forget in Boyle's case, especially since Boyle had been the only man at the chess tournament the first night to act like a human being.

Now Remo found himself looking at the gargantuan soles of the mammoth shoes on the heroic feet of the Rev. Robert A. Boyle, S. J. The Sorbonne. M.I.T. Anthropologist. Classical Scholar. Mathematician. Director of Bicycle Analysis at Brewster Forum.

Remo ran his mind back over the pornographic photos of Boyle. Yes, they had shown his giant feet. Remo had seen them, memorized them, but they had not registered. His perceptions were slipping. It was the three month peak. He was falling apart.

"Well?" Boyle had sat up at the desk and was looking at Remo.

"Well what?"

"I was wondering what you thought of our looney bin."

"A great place to visit. I wouldn't want to live here."

"Not much chance of that. Your presence here seems to have a deleterious effect on the quietude of our little rest home. First, making Ratchett look silly at the chess tournament. And then yesterday that show with those hooligans."

"It's what I get paid for," Remo answered laconically. Stop being a nice guy, he thought. Be a bastard. Then I can figure out a way to kill you, without any regrets.

"I'll have to ask you a lot of questions," Boyle said.

"Is there any reason I should answer them?"

If he had heard, Boyle ignored him. "I'll need to know where you were born and where you were brought up. Your native stock. All the usual dates and anniversaries. When you went to prison."

The alarm light flashed in Remo's mind. Prison? What did Boyle know ... what could he know ... about Remo's past? He forced himself into calmness. "Prison?" he asked casually. "What made you think I'd been in prison?"

"It's been my experience," Boyle said, his cool blue eyes looking guilelessly into Remo's hard face, "that people who are so quick tempered and so efficiently violent usually have seen the inside of a cage. At least in this country. In mine, we make them prime ministers."

"Well, that's one against you," Remo answered. "Never been in prison. At least, not in this life." Which was technically true.

Boyle made a note on a yellow pad with a stub of a pencil held in his big pink bricklayer's hands. He looked up again. "Shall we go on?"

"Can you give me a reason why we should?"

Boyle walked to a small refrigerator in a corner of his office. Remo declined a drink and Boyle poured himself a water tumbler full of Irish whisky. Alcohol abstinence was not one of his vows.

"Sure. It'll keep me on the job here and off the parish bingo circuit for another year."

"Fair enough."

By the time the tumbler of whisky was drained, Remo had learned that bio-cycle analysis was the study of rhythms in men's lives. Boyle contended that there were unconscious rhythms that determined behavior.

"If we can isolate those individual rhythms, we can understand behavior. Maybe even predict or control it."

Boyle showed Remo a bar chart. "See this line?" he asked pointing to a vertical bar. "Accidents per 10,000 driving hours in a Tokyo cab company."

"Now this line," he said, pointing to a shorter bar. "Accidents per 10,000 hours six months later. Why the difference?"

"They probably hired German hackies. You ever see Japs drive?"

An honest laugh fractured Boyle's tomatoed face. "No. Same drivers. But the company analyzed their body cycles and notified them to be careful on days that we call 'critical.' Just that, and the accident rate's cut in half. Follow me?"

"Maybe. What kind of cycles are there? Do they really control people? Do you really believe in this horseshit?"

Boyle went on to explain that after a half-century of study, scientists had isolated three cycles: a 23-day emotional cycle, a 28-day physical rhythm and a 33-day intellectual cycle. But now, with computers, science could absorb vast amounts of data on enormous numbers of people. "If we feed enough facts into the machinery, we may be able to detect totally new cycles and rhythms. Rhythms of love. Or hate."

"Why'd you want to talk to me?"

"Our basic study around here is violence. You're the first violent man we've had here in years. A rarity. Someone who doesn't intellectualize everything to death."

"Did you study McCarthy? The man I replaced?"

"Yes, I did. You know he was murdered, don't you."

Boyle was the second man to tell Remo that McCarthy had been murdered. He looked blankly at the priest. "No, I didn't know. I thought he committed suicide."

"Horseshit, to borrow your word. On the day he was killed, McCarthy was experiencing a very rare phenomenon. His emotional, physical and intellectual cycles all happened to coincide at a peak. It should have been the brightest day of his life. Men don't commit suicide on days like that."

"Who'd want to kill him?" Remo asked, watching Boyle's face carefully. "As far as I could find out, he wasn't mixed up in anything. Not like blackmail . . . or a porno ring."

Boyle showed no reaction at all. "Damned if I know who did him in. But I hope you find out who it was. McCarthy was a decent sort."

Boyle began to ask Remo a string of long, generally harmless questions about his life. Remo stuck to the fake biography of the fake Remo Pelham. Whenever Boyle got close to Remo's true past, to CURE, to his mission, Remo lied. It took over an hour.

Remo found he was in the fourth day of his emotional cycle, 18th day of his intellectual cycle and 15th day of his physical cycle. "That explains yesterday," Boyle said. "It was a day of physical crisis for you. Mid-cycle. You were passing from an up period to a down and were edgy.

If the whole thing had happened tomorrow, you would have turned your back and walked away. Unfortunate for those poor hooligans."

"For them? I might have been hurt."

"I rather doubt it," Boyle said.

Walking out into the courtyard from Boyle's cottage office, Remo was puzzled. So they were studying violence at the Forum. Big deal. Maybe Brewster's little plan to conquer the world involved talking your enemy to death. They sure as hell weren't going to figure out everybody's cycle and only fight when the rhythms were on our side.

And the pornographic pictures. That was another riddle. Boyle's blue eyes hadn't wavered when Remo mentioned blackmail or dirty photos. Remo was convinced Boyle knew nothing about the pictures. Yet he had obviously posed for them. Really posed, because the pictures were professionally lighted and shot from a number of different angles. And now he knew nothing about it.

If the word came, Boyle would have to be killed one-on-one. By hand. He had no repetitious habits, few hobbies, rarely left his cottage. It would have to be an accident in the house. Something with an electric cord perhaps. If the word came. Remo hoped it wouldn't.

CHAPTER TWELVE

When Remo was a boy, he had a fantasy of growing up to become the great white hunter. Whatever was left of the fantasy vanished when the rhinoceros charged and crushed the chained jackal under his 3,000 pounds of weight. The jackal left hardly a smear.

Remo continued to watch the film in fascination as the camera lens was changed and the rhino receded in the distance. Then, stepping into the film came Dr. Abram Schulter, his long, sparse black hair stringing down from a pith helmet. He carried a small black box, but it looked large in his birdlike hands.

He began to walk toward the rhino, shouting as he went. Occasionally he stopped and waved his helmet to try to attract the near-sighted beast's attention. When he was no more than thirty yards away, he stopped and began yelling again.

Finally, the rhinoceros charged. His hooves made the ground beneath the camera vibrate as he thundered from the right side of the screen toward the puny figure of

Schulter standing defenseless on the left side of the screen. Schulter looked up, seemed to watch the rhino for a split second, then flicked a switch on top of the box. The rhino stopped as if he'd run into an invisible wall.

He stopped dead and stood there, ten yards away from Schulter. Not moving. The film faded; the next frames showed the rhino lying down eating grass and Schulter sitting on its back. The beast couldn't have cared less.

Remo was impressed, but he couldn't resist a grin and the thought, this screwball will mount anything, toy giraffes, rhinoceroses, anything. Mothers in the neighborhood should lock up their rubber duckies.

The lights came on. Wearing a doctor's gown, Abram Schulter, M.D., Ph. D., Fellow of, Diplomate of, pioneer of this and that and everything else, came paddling toward Remo on ripple-soled shoes and began lifting the blinds to let sunlight into the darkened office.

"And so that's what we do," he said, as if the film explained everything.

"You mean, you're a rhinoceros trainer?"

"A rhinoceros trainer? No, why should I be? Oh yes, I see. A little joke. Yes, yes. Very good. Very good indeed."

He went on: "No, no. Electronic brain stimulation. The box in my hand was a radio. It sent a signal that stimulated alpha waves in the brain of the rhino. Such a brain as it has, that is. Alpha rhythms bring inner peace. Don't suppose you'd be interested?"

Schulter walked from the window and sat down on the other side of the coffee table facing Remo. He took a cigarette from a wooden box on the table and lit it. His hands were deeply nicotine stained, and like all compulsive smokers, he didn't offer Remo one.

Remo leaned forward and took one anyway, even

90

though it was a violation of his rules at peak. He lit it with a lighter on the table, and then put the lighter and the box back on Schulter's side of the table. He inhaled deeply, careful not to let the smoke change his breathing rhythm, exhaled for exactly two beats, and then looked at Schulter.

"I'm no rhinoceros. I'm not even a toy giraffe. What do you want with me?"

"Well, you know. I saw you in the yard with those silly-looking putzes. I mean. Such violence. I thought you might like to find inner peace. Would you?"

"Could I?"

"Certainly. All I would need to do is plant electrodes inside your skull. Very simple really."

"Has anyone ever offered to plant his foot up your ass?"

Schulter sighed. "Very common response. Not unusual at all." He puffed rapidly on his cigarette, then leaned forward, picked up the cigarette box, turned it in his hand as if examining it and then replaced it precisely in the center of the table. He did the same with the lighter.

"Well, at any rate," he said. "I just thought I'd ask. What I'd really like is to get the flow of your brain waves under stimulation. Very simple really."

"What kind of stimulation?," Remo asked.

"Just photos flashed on a screen," Schulter said.

"Why me?" Remo asked.

"Why not? You're new here. I've done everybody else." Schulter vanished into a large cabinet at the other end of the room, and came out bearing a metal half-helmet and a film cartridge that he placed in the movie projector.

The metal helmet had a long cord attached to it, which

91

Schulter plugged into a console panel on the other side of the room.

He flicked two switches and the round eye of an oscilloscope lit up with a hum at the top of the console.

"Helmet's an induction microphone really," Schulter said, handing it to Remo. "Instead of sound, it picks up tiny electrical impulses from your brain. They're visible on the scope," he said, pointing to the console, "and also on a paper tape. For record keeping."

Remo felt the helmet. He had seen one like it before. It had been lowered over his head when he was strapped into the electric chair at the New Jersey State Prison.

Schulter was still explaining. "You put the helmet on and watch the screen. Pictures appear, at prescribed intervals, and the tape records the change in brain pattern from the stimulus. Quite harmless."

Remo shrugged and sat in the chair. Gingerly, he lowered the helmet over his head and looked up at the screen. Flashing through his mind was a ritual of Chiun's. Chiun would sit in the lotus position and hum, a single steady low pitched note, that he claimed drained the brain and body of tension. Remo suspected that it stimulated the frequency of brain-calming alpha waves, perhaps through the direct vibration of the jawbone against the brain cavity, forcing the brain into producing them.

Schulter sat down at the console with his back to Remo. The oscilloscope was fully warmed now and its hum echoed through the room. Schulter flicked another switch and the film engaged. Remo cleared his brain of distractions and tried to emulate the low, humming note that he had heard Chiun emit many times.

A picture lit up the screen. A field of flowers gentled by the breeze, birds flying overhead in the sky. A control film probably to get a typical rested reaction from the subject against which the others could be compared.

Remo hummed, his sound masked by the oscilloscope.

After twenty seconds, the flower scene gave way to a splash of red. The camera faded back and the red turned out to be a blotch of blood on the white-shirted chest of a dead man, his eyes open, his face grinning idiotically.

Remo hummed.

The next picture showed Communist Chinese methodically gunning down Korean villagers standing against a wall.

Remo hummed.

The fourth scene showed a child cringing and then a burly man slapping the little child, hard, hard enough to make the child's head snap back and forth.

Remo hummed.

Schulter flipped a switch and the projector stopped. Others switches turned off the console. The scientist stood up and looked at the long string of paper tape in his hands. Remo stood up and took the helmet off.

"Did I pass?"

Startled, Schulter looked up. "Oh, yes. Yes. Quite good, really. Highly stable."

Remo tried to leer. "Maybe you should have showed me some pornography. Whips and boots. You know. That might have helped."

Schulter's reaction was none at all. If the helmet had been on his head, there would have been no change. Pornography was just a word to him. He knew nothing. Nothing about pornography. Nothing about toy giraffes. Nothing about a wild-eyed, black-haired woman with boots and a whip.

"Perhaps we'll do the test again. Most often, it's best."

"Well, perhaps some other time, Doctor."

Schulter waved Remo out of the cottage, absently, still studying the paper tape. He looked up as Remo left, staring at the broad back of the chief of security. Remo was smiling. And humming.

If the time came, he thought, Schulter would be easy. A wiring switch on the helmet and a tragic laboratory accident. A quite different sort of accident from the one which almost befell another Brewster Forum scientist, five minutes later, at the hands of Remo Pelham.

CHAPTER THIRTEEN

One inch and one-fiftieth of a second. Death had come that close to Anthony J. Ferrante, director of bio-feedback research at Brewster Forum.

Remo had knocked at the white cottage door bearing Ferrante's name and pushed the door open when a voice called "come in."

The desk facing the door was empty when Remo entered. His eyes scanned the room looking for Ferrante.

Did he hear the sound? Or did he sense the infinitesimal change in pressure as an air mass moved toward his left ear?

Remo pivoted to the left on the ball of his left foot. His right foot extended behind him and his body dropped into a deep crouch, in time to see a hand flashing down toward him in a karate slash.

There was no time to think, no need to think. Thousands of hours of training and practice had made defense automatic and retaliation instinctive. Remo's left hand flashed up to the side of his head to catch and deflect the

95

blow on his wrist. His right hand had already retracted to his hip, and without stopping had fashioned itself into the classical hand spear and was moving forward toward the left kidney of the man Remo had not yet seen.

Remo's breath exploded in a violent cry of "ai-ee" as his iron hand flashed on toward its target. As it finished its deadly course, Remo felt, rather than saw, his opponent's hand stop on its downward path before making contact. The man had pulled his punch.

Attack is instinctive, triggered by the spinal column, its message bypassing the brain and moving directly to the muscles. But calling off an attack? That is an act of intellect, belonging to the brain, and the brain was not swift enough to stop Remo's hand, to relax the braided rope muscles of his arm, to soften the intensity of these gently curled fingertips which could smash cinder blocks into powder.

Remo's brain did the best it could in one-fiftieth of a second. It changed the course of his hand one inch. The hand spear slid over the hip bone of his opponent, past the vulnerable kidney, and crashed into a wooden coat rack standing alongside his assailant. Fingers hit wood with the crack of a china dish splintering on a stone floor. The top half of the coat rack paused drunkenly, then fell to the floor, its two-inch thick wooden support split cleanly by the killing power of Remo's hand.

His opponent looked at the coat rack. Remo looked at his assailant for the first time and a saw a husky, middle-aged man wearing the classic judogi, a black sash wrapped low around his waist. He had a complexion like oiled olives. Dark rings surrounded his eyes, seeming even darker in contrast to his highly-glossed bald head. It was Ferrante.

Remo's left hand snaked out and snared Ferrante's

right hand. His thumb insinuated itself into a ganglion of nerves on the back of the hand, just alongside the base of the index finger. The move brought excruciating pain and immediate submission.

The man screamed. "Stop it. I'm Ferrante." His eyes met Remo's in pained, embarrassed truth.

Remo squeezed once more, then released the hand. "What the hell does that make you? The mugger in residence?"

"I wasn't going to hit you," Ferrante said, rubbing his damaged hand. "I just wanted to see how good you are. After yesterday." He looked at the fractured coat rack. "You're good."

Remo backed away to let the man move from the corner behind the door. He breathed deeply, slowly, to drain the tension, to allow his body to back off the heroic blast of adrenalin that had flooded his muscles.

Well, that was it. If the word came, Ferrante would die in the gymnasium of a broken neck, suffered in an incorrect judo fall. Remo would take great pleasure in bouncing him off a wall.

Ferrante walked slowly back to his desk, still rubbing his hand, eyes on Remo, spewing apologies. Remo began to feel sorry for the karate buff, for his pain, for his embarrassment. He wondered what Ferrante would think if he saw the pornographic photos of himself wearing only the top of his judo garb. If he hadn't seen them already.

Ferrante was still talking, still apologizing. "Look, it was stupid. How about if we forget it happened, and start all over? You're probably wondering why you're here. What we do here."

Remo grunted. He wasn't ready to forgive and forget yet.

"What we do here is study the mind. How it works. Each of us has a different discipline. Mine is bio-feedback. Basically that means using the pain-pleasure principle to train people to regulate their involuntary body functions. For instance, we've had some great success in training people to slow their pulse rate. If their rate goes too high, they receive a small electric shock. As their pulse rate drops toward the goal, they receive a pleasurable electronic impulse."

"What good is it?" Remo asked.

"Well, medically, it's very important. We could help save lives of people who are troubled with heart irregularities. Asthmatics could learn to will their way out of serious breathing attacks. Psychosomatic illnesses could virtually be wiped out." He was warming to his subject now.

As he talked on, Remo thought that Chiun should have been sent here to investigate this place. The aged Korean with his fishheads and rice and Zen could give all these big brains a run for their money. During those long training sessions, he remembered seeing Chiun slow his heart beat until it was almost imperceptible, his breathing rate until he appeared to be dead. Chiun had told Remo that Chiun's father could stanch the flow of blood by thinking about it. "The mind," he said. "You cannot control the body until you control the mind."

"Where did you learn to do it?," Ferrante intruded on Remo's thoughts.

"Do what?"

"The business with those shits out in the courtyard."

"Around. Correspondence courses. A one-hour workout every month whether I want to or not. Helps keep me in trim."

Ferrante had recovered his poise now. Still wearing the incongruous judo outfit, he was very much the world-renowned scientist.

He showed Remo the equipment he worked with, and

Remo thought that scientific equipment everywhere on every project is probably interchangeable. These fakers probably trade it around among themselves like used books. There was a chair with a hand grip through which a minor electric shock passed into the subject if he failed to respond and another helmet, like Schulter's, through which pleasurable waves passed by induction into the brain.

Ferrante was offering to test Remo. Well, I owe him one. I'll give him something to chew on. He sat in the chair and his resting pulse rate was sixty-eight. If the rate went up, Ferrante said, he'd get a slight shock through the hand grip. A down rate would bring a pleasure impulse through the helmet he placed over Remo's head.

Ferrante set a metronome at sixty-five beats per minute. "That's the goal," he told Remo, "but don't be disappointed if you don't make it. Hardly anyone does."

The metronome was ticking, Ferrante was holding Remo's wrist in a running check on his pulse, and Remo was remembering the trick Chiun had taught him. Set up your own rhythm, wipe out external impulses, speed up your breathing pattern to match the desired heart rate, and let the hyper-ventilation of the lungs slow the heart by flooding the blood with oxygen.

"Ready?," Ferrante asked. "I'll call out your heart rate as we go along so you can try to adjust."

"How bad's the shock?" Remo asked. "I'm afraid of electric chairs."

"Nothing to worry about," Ferrante said. "More like a buzz than a real shock. Start. . . . now."

The metronome was clicking its sixty-five beats per minute and Remo tuned his breathing pattern into it.

"Sixty-eight," Ferrante called. Remo quietly snorted his breath in and out.

99

"Sixty-six."

Remo closed his eyes to the metronome and blanked the sound of its rhythms out of his mind. He chose a new lower rhythm, and adjusted his breathing to it.

"Sixty-four." Ferrante was delighted. Remo breathed.

"Sixty."

"Fifty-nine."

Remo decided to call a halt when he had dropped his heart rate down to forty-two. Ferrante didn't know whether to be delighted or upset, or whether he had been cheated.

"That's incredible," he said. "I never saw anything like that."

"I told you, I'm afraid of electric chairs. And I've got a low tolerance of pain."

And then there was Ratchett. Remo never had a chance to figure out what Ratchett did, or how to get to him, because Ratchett refused to open the door to his cottage which, unlike the other top staff, he used only for an office, preferring to live in his eggshell home a few hundred yards away.

"Go away," he shouted. "I don't like you."

"I thought you wanted to see me," Remo told the closed door.

"If I never see you, it will be too soon. Go away."

"Must I assume, Doctor Ratchett, that you don't like me?"

"You will be well within the limits of possibility, Mister Pelham, if you assume that I loathe you. Now go away before I call a cop. One of your own will know how to deal with you."

Remo turned and walked away. Ratchett too would be easy if the call came. He did not realize that someone else would issue the call for Ratchett before CURE did.

CHAPTER FOURTEEN

Later that day, the staff department heads of Brewster Forum had held their regular weekly meeting in Brewster's office. Dr. Deborah Hirshbloom was absent.

Ferrante was talking about the new director of security. "So basically, he's a coward. Terribly afraid of pain. Just the threat of the electric shock produced an incredible swing in his pulse rate."

He sat down. Abram Schulter's chuckle broke the silence. "Inadequate data, Professor Ferrante. Incorrect analysis of the inadequate data. Mr. Pelham is fearless. Cold blooded! In brain wave analysis, he had absolutely no reaction to any of the external stimuli. None at all."

"Probably," Ratchett snarled, "you failed to have the machine plugged in. Did either of you consider that Pelham's intelligence is probably just too low to respond adequately to stimuli which is emotionally charged, but also intellectually powerful?"

"Is that your feeling?" Boyle asked. "That Pelham is of low intelligence?"

"Of course," Ratchett said. "Isn't it obvious? And think of his performance out in the courtyard with that awful gang. Is that a sign of intelligence?"

Boyle smiled. "I might suggest that there is more intelligence involved in chasing them away than there is in calling them here."

Ratchett flushed. Boyle went on. "I would say Mr. Pelham's intelligence is extremely high. He is also very devious and suspicious. He answers a question with a question. It's a yid trick—excuse me, Abram—but it's also the sign of a man used to intellectual sparing, who always looks for a quid before giving away a quo."

Nils Brewster listened quietly through all this, sucking on his pipe, his hands resting on his corpulent stomach, his nose encased in more bandage than was really necessary. If Brewster had a secret for his success, it was this: his ability to dominate a group, keep them splintered and leaderless and unable to challenge his authority. He finally spoke.

"Well," he said, "I suppose that settles it. Our new policeman is either very smart or very stupid. He is either a coward or absolutely fearless." He looked at all of them and sneered. "Another victory for intellectual analysis."

"This sounds curiously like the argument about whether a shark is brave, because he will attack anything no matter how big, or cowardly, because he prefers to feed off the crippled, the sick and the dying. Or is a lion clever, as he shows himself to be in his stalking of prey, or stupid, as he indicates by his irrational behavior when caged in a zoo?

"The fact is, as all of you should know by now, that the shark is neither brave nor cowardly. And the lion is neither clever nor stupid. They exist outside of these concepts. They are instinctual and those words are meaningless when applied to them. Did it ever occur to any of you that perhaps our tests are meaningless for Mr. Pelham, because they are designed for normal human beings? Did it ever occur to you that perhaps Mr. Pelham is like an animal, showing behavior patterns that once we would characterize as intelligent, another time as stupid; one time as brave, another time as cowardly? Did it ever occur to you that Dr. Pelham might be a creature of instinct or a human being programmed to act as a creature of instinct? And that to study him and understand him, we must approach him as we would approach a beast of the field?

"Did any of that every occur to any of you geniuses?"

He sat back and occupied himself with his pipe and with being Nils Brewster. No one else spoke. He puffed rapidly on his pipe, satisfied that he had again won the day, and then went on:

"Frankly, I don't know why any of us care about this Remo Pelham. I surely don't. But—just academically of course—I think he is perhaps best measured against the standards of instinct. Through his unconscious. It would seem to be the province of Dr. Hirshbloom. I suggest we just forget him, and let him go on doing whatever it is a policeman does around here. Leave him for Dr. Hirshbloom if she's interested.

CHAPTER FIFTEEN

But it was obvious that Dr. Hirshbloom did not wish to deal with the American. The new Brewster Forum bobby showered the little Hebrew wench with the typical colonial effusiveness that Americans consider charm, and civilized people understand as undue familiarity.

Geoffrey Hawkins, Brewster Forum sky-diving instructor, and former subaltern of Her Majesty's Royal Marines, refused to bestow the recognition of a glance upon either his pupil or that incredible American who insisted upon trying to make a date with her.

Hawkins sat in the Piper Cub, his parachute a cushion behind him and his legs stretched across the width of the small single-engine plane.

It was his job, a labor for daily purse, to instruct any staff members of the Forum who wished to parachute in the art of parachuting. Fortunately, that incredible motley crew of the gross technological giant that George III had allowed to wend its crude way into independence, dared not suffer Hawkins' explicit and daily disdain.

Only the Israeli girl, who undoubtedly had to continue her training, participated in the sky diving. Which was rather a bit of all right, since she had the decency not to attempt a conversation with Geoffrey Hawkins. Either she knew her place, understood decorum, or had nothing to say. Which for a Jew was an incredible virtue. Unfortunately so few other people shared her ability to refrain from conversation.

Like that typically German bore, who pretended to be of another nationality. He had given Hawkins $5,000 to see that Remo Pelham did not land alive. But then he had insisted upon trying to justify it to Hawkins.

Geoffrey Hawkins needed no justification. One had to live. And anyway, it would not be murder. Murder was when you deprived an Englishman of life. Survival was when you took life from an American. And public health was when one removed Irishmen.

It was a bit of a shame however that this Pelham was not Australian. Then one would know that one was removing a criminal. Or the seed of a criminal, which was the same thing anyway.

Even in Britain, the gentry had lost sight of what they were. The world had gone mad and Britain had gone mad with it. This pathetic affection and respect for America, a nation which had once had an Irish President. Scots walking around like human beings. Welshmen knighted every day. And all of them calling themselves British. When only Englishmen were English!

The sun had set on the soul of the British empire.

"Hey, buddy. How do you fix this thing?"

It was the American. He was going to jump from 13,000 feet, free fall for one minute, then open his chute and land. He had never been in a parachute before.

Five thousand dollars for this? Geoffrey Hawkins could

earn his money by allowing this colonial bumpkin just to attempt free fall. But that would not be thorough. *Thorough* was cutting the leg straps under the leather joints so that when the chute opened, if it opened, it would rise from the shoulder harness and Remo Pelham would keep going down, out of his chute, to the ground.

"Hey, buddy. How do you get this thing on?"

Geoffrey Hawkins turned to the financial pages. If one could properly invest one's $5,000, one could transform it into a rather considerable amount.

"Hey. You with the mustache and the paper. How does this thing buckle?"

Imperial Chemical Industries was up. Good. If one invested in Imperial Chemical Industries, one could not only help civilized industry but oneself. It was a good investment for oneself.

Finally, the Jewess helped him. No character, thought Hawkins. She had refused to talk to the American, had turned away from him, had ignored his blandishments and his insipid pleading, but now she turned to help him with the chute. Leg straps, shoulder straps, the rip cord ring, proper harness position.

When done, she turned away again. "Thirteen thousand feet," she said to Hawkins.

"Umm," he replied, because as jump instructor, he had to.

"We're ready," she said. The soon-to-be-dead American sat beside her.

The Germans had a point. But they were so crude about it. If one were to strip a German to his soul, one would achieve the essence of gauche. Even the way that Hun had slipped the envelope to Geoffrey Hawkins. As if he were reaching surreptitiously into Hawkin's privates.

"Yessir, this is going to be fun," said the American. His

brown eyes were shining. His face was shaved of hair. He would clunk like a pinball machine on the Virginia countryside. He would tilt in all directions.

The engines revved, groaning for power, and the light plane shook.

Her Majesty's forces, according to the Times, were still in Aden by the Persian Gulf. Lucky Aden. But this was America which had so stubbornly insisted upon going it alone and was paying for it daily.

The Jewess had finally relented. She was explaining something to the American. Hawkins listened from behind the *Times*.

"The plane is going to 13,000 feet. It's a one-minute free fall. You pull your cord immediately. Just follow me. I'll make sure your cord is pulled. You're very stupid trying this the first time."

"Listen, sweetheart, don't worry about me."

"You are incredibly stupid."

"This was the only way I could get to talk to you."

"As I said, you are incredibly stupid."

The two were yelling now, to overcome the motors.

"I want to talk to you," the American said.

"Your leg straps are too loose."

"When can we get together?"

"I'm busy this year. Try me next year at the same time."

Suddenly her voice called out, "Mr. Hawkins! Who gave him this chute?"

She was doing it again. Talking to Geoffrey Hawkins without being addressed first. He ignored her.

"Will you put down that paper? You can't let this man jump in this chute."

Put down the paper? What gall.

Suddenly the dark columns of small type disappeared.

107

The paper went flying. It had been ripped out of his hands by the American.

"I beg your pardon," Geoffrey said in his most disdainful manner, calculated to set the American cringing in apologies.

"Perfectly all right," the American responded. "She's talking to you."

"I am perfectly capable of discerning such auditory phenomena as women speaking. I do not need your assistance."

"Then why didn't you answer her?"

"That is hardly a topic I wish to discuss with you," said Geoffrey Hawkins to the American policeman. "Now return my *Times* if you would."

"Who gave him this parachute?," the girl asked. "Did you?"

"I am not a supply sergeant. I do not dispense parachutes."

"Well, he can't jump out of the plane in that chute."

"He certainly can't jump without one," said Hawkins, who thought that incredibly funny, worth repeating to an Englishman.

"It's no wonder the British army dispensed with your services," the girl said.

That was enough. Geoffrey would have to thrash her. He gave her the back of his hand across her face. At least, he attempted to. But it seemed as though some fast air current spun his hand harmlessly in the air.

"Keep your tongue, Jewess," he said, watching his hand flail to the side of the plane.

"Don't give me that shit, Hawkins. Did you unload the faulty chute on him?"

"Answer her," said the American.

The pilot interrupted. "We're approaching target and

108

13,000 feet," he called out. Good, that would settle everything. To jump from 13,000 feet one had to be in an aircraft that climbed almost straight up, and one jumped at its zenith. It was the only practical way, since if the plane levelled off at 13,000 feet, everyone would need oxygen. This way, the plane was at that altitude so briefly that oxygen was unnecessary.

"Jump, Dr. Hirshbloom, if you're going to," Hawkins said. The door near his feet opened, and the girl half stood up. As she struggled over Hawkins' outstretched legs, she said: "Don't let him jump in that chute." She turned to the American: "Don't you jump."

She thrust a boot out on to the strut, waited a moment, and was gone.

"Are you jumping, Yank? Or are you going to be typical and wait for a computer to do it for you?"

"I don't think I'll jump," said the American. The ripping wind from the open door whipped through his brown hair.

"Well, it's your choice," Hawkins said. "Here, why don't you have a look? You'll know what it's like next time. Or are you afraid to look."

"I know what the ground looks like, sweetheart," the American said.

"The Jewess makes an interesting jump," Hawkins said, peering out the door. "She does a very special free fall."

The American cop shrugged, stepped over Geoffrey's legs, and peered out. Geoffrey Hawkins put his shoulder to the American's back, braced his feet against his seat, and pushed hard, devastatingly hard. And nothing happened.

"You want to jump with me?," said the American, turning.

Geoffrey Hawkins pushed again and this time he was

109

successful. Too successful. He found his own energy, with an assist from the American, had hurtled him head first toward the wing struts outside, and then he was outside the plane, dropping through the chill cold wind, with the American firmly latched to his throat.

They accelerated quickly, then hit top speed and they were free falling. The American was smiling and humming Yankee Doodle.

Geoffrey attempted to kick him away. The $5,000 was as good as his. But the kick went nowhere. As a matter of fact, the right leg went out, and then became numb. The American's hands seemed to float, then dart, then plunge forward and back. And for all Geoffrey Hawkins' effort, he could not unlatch the colonial who just smiled and hummed and moved his hands in those extraordinary ways. Geoffrey attempted to use a karate chop against the bridge of the American's nose.

But as his hand started to move, it became numb, and then. . . . Ye gads. The left rider to the chute was slipping off the useless left hand. Then the American worked at the main buckle on the chest strap and it was off, and Geoffrey was suddenly spinning around and facing away from the American. Then the other strap to the right rider was eased off a suddenly numb right arm, and only his legs remained strapped into the unopened chute. And then Geoffrey was spinning again, this time face forward and he felt the chute yank up between his legs and he was diving head first towards the ground, without his parachute or the use of his limbs. He attempted to flip over, but there was just the slightest slap on his back and he remained, going face down, floating down.

Gads! He had no parachute. He was stripped of his chute. Then he felt himself being flipped up and there was the American face-to-face with him as they descended. He

110

was snapping on the buckle over the chest. He was wearing Geoffrey's parachute. He was smiling and still humming.

Geoffrey saw a khaki bundle thrust toward him. It was the American's faulty chute. Then the American shouted: "That's the biz, sweetheart. Remember me to Henry the Eighth."

Red and white material sprung out and up from the American's back, and then snapped into a ballooning canopy of an open chute. The American seemed to rise and then become farther and farther away as he swung from the riders in gentle descent.

Geoffrey Hawkins, late of Her Majesty's Royal Marines, arrived at the lush Virginia countryside at approximately the same moment as the faulty parachute. The chute bounced with a whoomph and was usable again.

Geoffrey Hawkins didn't. And wasn't.

By the time Remo landed, Doctor Hirshbloom had gone.

CHAPTER SIXTEEN

Brewster Forum had supplied Remo with a room in a two-story house, centrally located in the forum's laboratory complex and just as centrally out of sight of any of the private homes. It was called the workers' house.

"If you get lost, just ask for the workers' house," said the superintendent of the gymnasium.

"You mean we live here."

"Not we. I'm a superintendent. I have a home. The lower-level work force uses the workers' house. The cleaning women, drivers, cleanup men, security officer."

"Okay," Remo had said, "this will be fine." His room allowed him to dress standing up if he stood on the bed, and if he chose, jump right from the shower to his sheets. He could also use the two top drawers of the dresser, the bottom ones being wedged shut by the box springs of the mattress.

It was not really that the room was so small, but that the bed was so big. It had been a discard from one of the private homes and like all the furniture in the workers' house, was not designed for its room. Remo could do a somersault on the mattress, which he judged would cover three ordinary beds.

"That mattress alone cost $1400," one of the maids confided to him. "We're always getting furniture and stuff the people don't want. It's real good stuff, only sometimes it looks kind of funny."

Naturally Remo could not do his more exotic exercises in the Forum gymnasium, assuming that the continued sustaining of peak had not drained his abilities too much to do them at all.

But he could always exercise in the bed on his back, which might be enough. He stared at the ceiling and set his mind on a long road that had wound around the inside of the walls at Folcroft Sanitarium where he had received his first training. He mentally stepped out onto the black gravel path and felt the wetness of the air coming in off Long Island Sound and smelled the stale after-odor of the burnings of yesterday's leaves and he was off. Five quick miles today.

Looking at Remo in the bed at Brewster Forum, one would see only the leg muscles twitching and the chest moving regularly with the heavy breathing. In fact, it was the breathing that made the run worthwhile, and when he approached the last lap he began to sprint, pressing his deadened legs, gasping for breath and pushing, pushing, pushing. He had always been able to do the last lap with speed. But this morning the legs were just not there and the energy needed for the sprint couldn't be called up. He did not allow the thought that he might not be able to finish the final lap, although he did not know for sure how he could make it, and the pain became unendurable. He had not had so much trouble since he first began running.

He never did find out if he could finish. There was a

113

knock on the door of his room in the workers' house of Brewster Forum. Remo heard it and not wanting to open the door in an exhausted condition, went into a recover. Fortunately, he was in bed, the process being a complete nothing. Abandon all nerves, senses and muscles, drop all controls. Become a vegetable. The effect on the body was like an electric shock in water. The trick was to do everything simultaneously, because the heart could miss a beat, and if the rest of the system were still coursing through heavy exercise, it might not pick up that beat.

But it did, and Remo, sweat-drenched, but breathing like he had just awakened from a sleep, answered the door. He knew that the normal breathing, the lack of a heat-flushed appearance, would make the perspiration appear like water.

The man in the door was late middle-age, but his face was fleshy with hard lines, strangely unbroken by his round metal-framed eyeglasses. He wore a dark summer suit with white shirt and black tie, and offered a truly mechanical smile, the non-joyous likes of which Remo had not seen since the last Presidential campaign.

"Excuse me," said the man, with a polishing of gutturals in his voice. "I am Martin Stohrs, your chess instructor. I did not realize you were in the shower. I am sorry."

"No," said Remo. "I was trying to unstop the sink."

"And it exploded?"

"In a way."

"I don't imagine you can invite me in?" He was looking at the bed-filled room. "More like a bed with a room around it, no?"

"Yes."

"Terrible. Terrible. A man of your talent and abilities living in a room like this next to the servants."

114

"It's okay with me."

"Terrible. This should be outlawed. Security work in every place in the world is an honored profession requiring the highest of abilities and courage and discipline. And they put you here. I will speak to Brewster about this."

"He put me here."

Stohrs changed the subject. "I came to invite you to my house for the honor of a game with you, and if you would also honor me, I would appreciate your company at dinner. I had mentioned the game the other day when you had finished with those motorcycle swine, but you probably did not hear me."

"Thanks anyway, I have a date."

"So soon?"

"Well, it's sort of business. One of the staff. Doctor Hirshbloom."

"Ah, Deborah. Surprising. She rarely sees anyone. Unusual when you consider that this is a think tank, and what fills the tank mostly is words and more words." He seemed charmed by his joke.

"I'm not sure what this is."

"Hah, no one else is either. I like you. We must play."

"Thanks again, but some other time. I'm on my way to see someone now."

"Ach. Excuse me, most assuredly. The invitation is open."

Remo thanked him again and shut the door. He dressed in a pair of white chinos and a blue sports shirt. His two suits hung in the bathroom, the closet door not having room enough to open.

Stohrs was waiting downstairs. He was apologetic. He had not wished to intrude on Remo Pelham. He was not the pushy type like some people. He was not the pushy type for the mile and a half walk to the circle of cottages. He made that clear several times.

"You see, I come from a culture that appreciates privacy, just as it appreciates the true role of the policeman. You have violence in this country today because the policeman is not respected. Order is not respected. Now, in my country, no policeman would ever be forced to live in the servants' quarters when a golf instructor lives in a house. Yes?"

"Yes, what?" asked Remo, noticing how the night came unexpectedly fast for the summer. Or was it his imagination, or even worse, the losing of touch with time and senses and feeling. He did a toe walk so smoothly that he knew Stohrs did not notice and thus reassured himself that he could still do special things and therefore need not worry about his senses. It was the night.

"Yes, do you agree with me?"

"Certainly," Remo said. He began working his fingers, in a dexterity drill, playing speed. You separated the coordination of the hands, then played finger tip against fingertip, with the nails of the hand just touching, then retreating. Done quickly enough, it looked like nervous praying.

"These are terrible times we live in. No?"

"It's always a terrible time."

"Not always. And not everywhere."

"You could say that."

"You must like this place. And to like this place you must come from a place that is not so nice, yes?"

"Are you asking me where I'm from?"

"No, no. Of course not. I mean unless you wish to tell me."

"I don't particularly."

"Good. You will find that I am not the prying type. I

116

am just one who respects excellence. I respected your chess play. Where did you learn to play?"

"From Delphurm Bresky, a lawyer in Jersey City," Remo said, making up a name he knew couldn't exist.

"Then you are from Jersey City. A wonderful town."

"Jersey City, a wonderful town?"

"Well, it's gone down since that wonderful mayor you had."

"Who?"

"Francis Hague."

"That bum was a dictator."

"Yes. A terrible man. You worked long in Jersey City?"

"No."

"A short time?"

"No."

"Ah. You never worked there. Well, I am not one to seek a person's resume the first time I meet him. Especially not someone I like and respect, who has been abused by the powers that be. I am here only to offer my help."

Remo worked the shoulders and neck, using Stohrs as a foil. If he could do the control exercises just beneath Stohrs' level of awareness, it would be a good feedback check.

"You know, there are some civilizations that adore men of violence."

"Yeah. Most," Remo said. "The others become vassal states."

"Right. You are a man of the world," Stohrs said, slapping Remo's back in joy. It was unfortunate that Remo at the time was doing rapid mental jump pushups during his stroll. Remo's was the first back Stohrs had ever slapped that slapped back.

117

"You look surprised," Remo said.

"No. Nothing. I just thought that my hand hurt."

"That'll happen if you go around slapping people on the back."

"It was a sign of respect. It is terrible today that we do not have respect where we should have respect. In my country, we always have respect. That is what makes my country great. Always great, no matter what."

"What country is that?"

"Switzerland."

"A fine country. The best foreign policy in the world."

"Yes. Its mountains are its foreign policy."

"Very well put," Remo said.

Stohrs shrugged it off as a nothing.

"Strange," Remo said, "but mountains act as barriers and water as a conduit. Look at England. A little island that chose not to use its water as a barrier but as a vehicle to carry empire. Now, they're pretty much back on their island."

"The Britishers are overrated."

"They did pretty well at one time. For a small island."

"Well," Stohrs said, his voice rising. "Well. Who the hell did they ever beat? Napoleon? He was a sick man. A dying man. They beat him when he was dying. No. The Britishers get others to fight for them."

"They did pretty well in World War I and II."

"They didn't win those wars."

"They didn't lose them."

"They had almost nothing to do with them. America and Russia won those wars. The British were like the French, little toadies currying your favors. You are being used by the British. They laugh at you behind your back. Don't you see that?"

"I was never aware that America was laughed at."

118

"Laughing stock of the world. Of course, nothing personal."

"Of course not," Remo said. "It must be nice to come from a country protected by mountains, a country that neither gives aid nor receives it, a country whose only function is to be the world's counting house."

"It's a nice little country," Stohrs said. "Not a great country but a nice one. I am proud to call it home."

"What brings you here?"

"This is a lovely job and place to work. A good environment for me to raise my daughter. Lovely. That is, if you are not a policeman, no?"

"No," said Remo who had finished his mental situps and now saw that the light was on in the Hirshbloom cottage. "Good night and thank you for walking with me."

"It's an honor. I respect you. Watch your step. There is evil here. That tragic Hawkins' accident. I am glad we now have a real man as security officer.

"Real man?"

"Yes. I do not like to dishonor the dead, but McCarthy was just ... well, a clerk. You need a man for the job. Good night. We must play soon."

"We will."

And Remo would not see him again until he would defeat him at the chess table with only a king and queen, against a queen, a king, two knights, a rook and a bishop. It would be a brilliant move, one that no chess master could ever perform as well.

CHAPTER SEVENTEEN

The man once known as Dr. Hans Frichtmann sat in one of the foam-contoured seats of the Brewster Forum auditorium watching the weekly amateur show. They changed the program from week to week. Last week, it was Father Boyle on guitar; the week before that, Professor Ferrante in elegiac poetry. They never called it an amateur show and at first had attempted to sell tickets. The first week they sold eight, the next week six, and then they stopped charging.

He could see that the new director of security and Dr. Deborah Hirshbloom were among the missing. Well, that was something. It was undoubtedly a better performance than Dr. James Ratchett, his magic, and now his hypnotism.

He was frankly worried. The business with the motorcycle hoodlums was one thing. But how had he escaped the fall from the plane and managed to kill Hawkins in the process? He wished only that his job were finished. That he could leave this accursed place.

His attention was brought back to the stage by Ratchett's voice.

Dr. Schulter was sitting in a chair at center stage. Ratchett's lardy body was frozen before the seated figure. It had taken six minutes to put Schulter under, and the boredom of moving bodies coughing and sighing could be felt, as only courtesy tethered the forum personnel to their seats.

"Black longing pools of opalescent nights and the deepest of deep escapes. You are moving down, blackward, into darkness and restful slumber," Ratchett's voice purred. A few coughs brought a haughty condemning glance from Ratchett and back to the gibberish. Strange that a theoretical chemist, surrounded by great psychiatrists and psychologists, would seek to entertain them with hypnotism. And such amateurish hypnotism.

Oh, well. The dangers of espionage this decade varied. Death by boredom was a possibility. He heard Ratchett call for a return to horrible times. What were horrible times? Let's see. The surrender was bad, the Russian occupation worse. The removing of testicles from trembling men with forceps? Not bad at all, especially when that Jew professor stood before him. The Jew professor who had attempted to expel him from medical school in Hamburg because of alleged sadistic practices. What was wrong with sadism? Really. If you didn't look at it in the sloppy Jewish sentimentality, or through the rose-colored filter of Jewdom's whore child, Christian ethics. Sadism was good. It was the extension of natural hostility, to a point where it had its own meaning, its own beauty. The Nazi Party knew it.

The Nazi party. The only healthy, honest force in history. And the way these scrawny, hairy youngsters dared call the American government fascist and Nazi. How dare they? The American government, nothing but hypocritical flotsam, mealy-mouthing its way through history, obsessed with domestic well-being and international public opinion. How dare they call that Nazi? He could show them NAZI. They should see NAZI! They should see that Jewish professor. Why didn't that semitic scum scream? That was the bad part. He didn't scream. Yes. That was a horrible time. Horrible. As on stage.

Schulter was searching, in his hypnotic past, for a horrible time. Then he jumped to his feet, dancing around the stage. Skip and a hop. And his jacket flew to the floor, followed by his shirt, his undershirt. Unzip the pants and step out. Then down on his bony knees. The white stage-light reflected blue off his perspiring back. "The whip," he cried. "The woman with the whip. Whip. Whip."

Ratchett was panting heavily. "The whip," he chorused. "The whip," making little sucking noises through his puffy lips.

The staff was not sure what happened next. Nobody could recall exactly. But when the new director for security asked around the next morning, the story was this:

1) The hypnotism show had touched off something that was better not talked about and really none of Remo Pelham's business.

2) Dr. Nils Brewster snapped both men out of their trance by jumping on stage and mimicking Ratchett's voice.

3) Everyone was strangely disturbed by the episode, and really, stop bothering people.

They would be bothered though—even more, when they discovered the awesome price Doctor Ratchett would have to pay for his dramatic success.

CHAPTER EIGHTEEN

Having been thrown out of a plane while trying to talk to Dr. Hirshbloom, there was no price too great for Remo to pay to see her. He would even talk to Nils Brewster.

Brewster was arrogant, almost as if that tragic accident to the sky-diving instructor had been Remo's fault.

"No," Nils Brewster had said, through bandaged nose. "No request from Doctor Hirshbloom. Why are you so interested?"

"Why is there joy in your voice?"

"Don't answer a question with a question. They tell me that's how you carry on a conversation."

"Four out of five department heads want to talk to me. The fifth doesn't. Why?"

"That's your answer?" Brewster asked.

"Yes," said Remo.

"I told you you'd never understand about us."

"Well, I'm going to see her."

"You don't have my permission."

"How do I get it?"

"You don't."

"Do you know that if I flick your nose with this forefinger," Remo said, bringing the forefinger very close to the white bandages, "I can cause you all sorts of hurt?"

"And you'll be out on your ass before the throbbing subsides."

"What if a brick should fall on it at night from you know not where?"

"You'll be out on your ass before it hits the ground."

"What if I teach you to do to people what I did to those motorcycle thugs?"

"I'm pushing sixty, man."

"I could teach you to do it to at least two people."

"Young people?"

"Young people."

Dr. Nils Brewster dialed his telephone and said into the receiver: "Deborah, I thought you would like to do an input feedback on Remo Pelham, the new security officer. The others have and . . . oh. Yes, of course. Certainly I understand." He returned the telephone to the receiver.

"She said she was busy on something else. But you have my permission. I'll deny it afterwards, but of course that'll be too late. At least you're not risking your job. Now when do we start on the. . . ." Brewster made striking motions at young faces and young stomachs, dodging very swift punches of young athletes whom he would now rend asunder should the little twerps dare make wiseass comments on the road or in restaurants or anywhere. Anywhere.

"In two weeks."

"Two weeks?" Brewster looked hurt, cheated.

"Well, you've got to get into shape first. Run a quarter of a mile a day for a week, then a half-mile the following week."

"Anything else?"

"No. That's it."

"What is your school of attack, by the way? Karate, kung fu, judo?"

"Wow tu," said Remo, making up the most idiotic name he could think of.

"Wow tu? Never heard of it."

"That's why it works so well. Do you think anything really good would be sold out of a gymnasium or a book?"

"Wow tu," repeated Dr. Nils Brewster, Faversham Fellow of Sociology, Ph.D., University of Chicago, author of "Man as Hostile Environment."

"Wow tu," he said again, and in the place where dreams are formed he saw his older daughter's latest boyfriend crumple to the floor in agony.

Now Remo was at her cottage. Mosquitoes and moths held a mass rally near her window and Remo slapped unsuccessfully at them while awaiting her answer. He knocked again.

"Who is it?"

"Your security officer, Remo Pelham."

"What do you want?"

"I want to talk to you."

"About what?"

"I don't want to talk out here."

"Come back tomorrow."

"Can I see you now?"

"No."

"Are you busy?"

"Will you go away!" It was not a question.

"I just want to talk to you."

There was silence and the bugs poured in reinforcements. It was the stale hot of the Virginia summer, a deadening sweat-demanding night that buzzed with the insects of the land. And she did not answer.

"I'm not going until you talk to me."

"Does Brewster know you're bothering one of his scientists?"

"Yes."

"He does not. That is a lie. Leave me alone."

"After you talk to me."

He heard footsteps pad to the door. It opened, and Deborah Hirshbloom stood before him with the unamused tolerance of a parent declining to be manipulated by the antics of a child. Her face was set, but calm, enhancing its fine smooth lines. Her eyes were black jewels in a setting of smooth, milky skin garnished with the joy of freckles. Her lips, unpainted, were tight; allowing nothing for Remo standing before her.

"All right. What?"

"I'd like to talk to you. May I come in?"

"It's late."

"I know. May I come in?"

She shrugged and beckoned Remo to enter. She wore a plain khaki blouse with plain khaki shorts. She was barefoot, and her cottage office was just as bare, except for the books stacked to the ceiling and a chess set open on the small table, near the lamp. There was a metal cot and two chairs. She sat on the cot, but with such stiffness that it obviously was not an invitation.

"May I sit down?" Remo asked, nodding to the chair.

She allowed it.

"As you know, the other department heads of the forum have been interviewing me." She did not respond. Remo continued: "And I wondered why you had not."

"Because I'm not interested."

"I was, well, sort of wondering why."

126

"Because one man beating up seven ridiculous hoodlums is not exactly the awe-inspiring scientific phenomena my colleagues obviously believe it to be."

"Then you know something about violence."

"I am learning from you, and I like no part of it. I know Hawkins came down with your chute and you with his. I know he tried to kill you and died for it."

"You're Israeli, aren't you?"

"Yes. You know that."

"And violence offends you?"

"Yes."

"Don't all Israelis have to serve in the Army?"

"Yes."

"And violence still offends you?"

"Of course, why not?"

"Because you people couldn't survive without violence. Without being tough. The Arabs could have peace by not firing a shot. You people would have another holocaust."

"Mr. Pelham, what are you driving at? That because we are outnumbered one-hundred-fifty to one by people who unfortunately have made our annihilation a national goal, that I should like what I must do to survive? One must dig latrines, too, for survival. But you do not have to like digging latrines. What do you really want? You do not care that violence offends me. This does not interest you. What do you want?"

"Well, I have a problem and you contribute to it. You see, I'm responsible for the protection of everyone here. And everyone moves around so much, especially you, that to really make sure I can provide the proper security, I have to know generally where I can reach you when I need you. That attack on the forum by the motorcycle gang could be a portent of things to come. I'm not sure

127

they will, but if those people try again, I want to make sure they can't reach any of the top staff."

"There is a word in English, Mr. Pelham, that describes beautifully what you have just said. It is both sharp in definition and meaningful in substance."

Remo knew he was opening a door. "What word?" he said, preparing himself for the deserved consequences.

"Bullshit," said Dr. Hirshbloom sweetly.

"That's unfair, Deborah."

"That is your name, Remo, it is bullshit should you deny it to your grave. They called for you. They challenged you. And they got you. Or, as you will, you got them."

"They went for me first so that they could get to you. Certainly you are aware of a situation like that. Russia attacking us through Israel."

"Why must you put everything on an international level? You're sitting here, asking my schedule, obviously not to protect me because you know I do not need your protection. So why else would you want to know where you can reach me, except to do me harm? Right?"

"Bullshit."

"Hah. Mr. Pelham. . . ."

"Remo, remember."

"All right, Remo. Good night."

"Deborah, I would like to see you again."

"I'm certain you will. But, please. Not in such frightening fashion as the other day, or such annoying fashion as tonight."

"Frightening? You were frightened? You didn't seem frightened?"

"Now I am terrified because now I know you even had time to look around at me and the other scenery." Deborah sat calm, but a cool formal smile set it. It did not

128

change, and Remo recognized the personal control people develop when they are faced frequently with danger. They develop it, or they die, or they are incredibly lucky.

"All right. I had time to look around. Suppose that is so. Suppose my defense was really an attack. Suppose all those things."

"Then suppose, Mr. Pelham, you're not a policeman."

"All right, suppose that."

"Then you must be something else."

"Then I'm something else."

"Then I don't feel comfortable. I do not feel comfortable, seeing an approach to attack which I recognize, and then seeing added an awesome ability to do things that I do not recognize at all. I was truly afraid the other afternoon, Mr. Pelham. And I was afraid of you. I am afraid of you now."

"Strange for a psychiatrist."

"I am tired also, Mr. Pelham. Good night. I do not know what you are really here for. Perhaps it is even to be, as you say, a security officer. But I have seen your like before. When I was a little girl, a volunteer from America. He taught us that set, and two days ago I saw it on you."

Chiun in Israel? Impossible. The set? It was not Chiun who taught the set, the apparently awkward foot alignment that made you look as if you were about to step backward when really you moved forward. That was not Chiun. The first days of training after the electrocution were. . . . Of course, the set. Conn MacCleary. Conn MacCleary in Israel?

Deborah rose to usher Remo to the door. Remo remained seated.

"This man, did you like him?" Remo asked.

"As a matter of fact, the whole village loved him. But he is dead now, a fate that awaits us all. It is really only a

129

question of when. And toward extending that *when,* we are all devoted, no?"

"Where did this man die?"

"You seem very interested in this man. Why?"

"Perhaps I knew him."

"If you did I would not have to fear you anymore because he was a good man. That is what we all remembered about him most. He was a good man. What he did for his livelihood does not attract good men that often. He was rare. And he died. And I believe he probably died sooner than he should. Because good men do not often live long lives in some situations."

Her voice was softer now and Remo detected a break, the quiver of emotion stronger than one expects, a memory that remains forever too fresh.

"This good man," Remo said, "had he lost a hand?"

"Yes," said Deborah.

"And was his name Conn MacCleary?"

"Yes," said Deborah, and she shut the door she had opened. "You knew him then?"

"Yes," said Remo. "I knew him."

"You were in the American intelligence then?"

"No, no," Remo said. "I knew him. I knew him once."

"Do you know how he died?"

"Yes."

"They said it was in a hospital."

"It was. It was. In a hospital."

And Deborah's face became a smile and warmth and tenderness, a delicate joy that people who can understand beautiful things bestow upon their surroundings.

"It is funny, and since you remember Conn, so typical," she said, taking the chair facing Remo. "When he came to our village, it was just before independence when the five Arab armies attacked, and we had, I think, one

130

rifle for five men in our village, or something like that. I was very young."

"Of course," Remo said.

"Of course," Deborah laughed. "Well, he had volunteered to give special training to people, I am not at liberty to disclose what, and we were all waiting for him. Anxious. Everybody was anxious. My uncle would say: 'When the American arrives here, he will show you all what technology is. Wait and see. American organization.' So it is supposed to be a big secret and so naturally everybody knows about it and is waiting for his arrival. Like a welcoming committee for his secret entrance into our village. Well, he is driven up in the back of a car, and I do not know if you know how valuable a car was to us then, but you can imagine, and Conn is in the back seat and you will never guess. . . ."

"He was drunk," Remo supplied matter of factly.

Deborah guffawed and slapped Remo's knee. Tears began to form in her eyes and she struggled to talk through the laughter.

Remo added quickly: "Sure. I told you I knew Conn MacCleary."

And his casual way of saying this threw Deborah into an hysterical reach for the table to steady herself. "Drunk," she finally said. "He was passed out drunk. You should have seen the look on Uncle David's face. He kept asking the driver if this was the right man and the driver kept nodding. We found out later he had been drinking since Tokyo where he had been mustered out, I think it was a month before. Drunk? He reaked. I mean when they carried him out everyone stepped back he smelled so badly."

"Conn MacCleary," Remo said.

131

"He was one of a kind. It took him three days to realize where he was."

"There must have been a lot of pressure then."

"Well, not really so much for us. Our training thing was for something else. I think we all believed that we would win. Although it was frightening and I was, at the time. . . ."

"After all, a young girl."

"Of course. Otherwise I would be an old woman instead of the incredibly attractive, beautiful young woman that I am now."

"Of course. You know you are beautiful."

"Come. Stop that. I gave you a MacCleary story. Now you give me one."

"Well, the first time I saw Conn," Remo said, conveniently planning to leave out details, "was. . . . No, let me see. The first time."

"No. The second time," Deborah said. "The first you won't tell me and that's all right. So tell me the second time."

Okay. So she believed he was with the CIA or the FBI. So what? That was to be expected from the kind of work they were doing here anyway. He had used CIA as a cover before anyhow.

"Okay," Remo said. "I was coming-to in a hospital bed and he was wheeling in this great dinner with lobster and booze."

"For someone in a hospital bed?"

"This is Conn MacCleary we're talking about."

"Yes," Deborah agreed with a nod.

"And he lays out this beautiful spread, abuses the doctor and nurse, tells me to eat up. And he drinks all the booze."

"Conn MacCleary," Deborah said in punctuation.

"But that's not the half of it. I never knew the man to be away from a bottle for long. It's a wonder he lived past twenty-one."

"The Egyptians are making a push up through the Negev. We're near there."

"Where?"

"Never mind. Will you let me finish? Besides, none of that stuff about wheres. Read my official biography if you want to know wheres."

"I bet they're the wrong wheres."

"Stop that shit, Remo. Just stop and listen. Because if you want to play question and answer with me, I can go to Dr. Brewster and complain about nasty interference from you agents-kind-of-people, and he'll beat you within an inch of your life. Hah."

"Okay. No more shit."

"Okay. We are near the action and Conn is desperately gathering copper tubing. Uncle David says, 'Hah. You see. Secret weapon. I told you. Technology. American technology.' And Conn is being very secretive. No one can go near where he is preparing his technology. One day I followed him. And there behind some rocks, sandbagged . . . let me tell you, sandbagged . . . we should have that kind of defense on the Suez Canal today . . . it looks like he has emptied the Sinai into burlap. He had all the children stripping the entire village of sandbags for this. And my Uncle David was leading it. Sandbags for the secret weapon of our village. Well, since it is so top secret no one is allowed to look. But I look. I knew he would not punish me. I was his favorite, but he loved all the children."

"Con love children?"

"Oh yes. That was his big love, I believe. And I believe

133

because he never had children was why he drank. He would tell us stories at night. We all loved him."

"Conn? Children?"

"Shut up. Let me finish. I crawl over the sandbags and I peek. There he is with a cup underneath this copper tubing which is all twisted and connected to a small boiler. He had made a still and I can't describe him waiting for the drip, drip, drip with the cup. This grown man, bending over in this incredible heat made hotter by the sandbags, the defense of our village by the way, just waiting for the drip, drip, drip."

Remo shook his head. "Yeah, that's Conn. But I can't imagine his stripping a village's defense for it."

"Well, the sandbags were not really that important, and he knew that within a half hour for every bag he got, it would be replaced. We were not short of sand."

"Tell me though. What happened there to make him hate the Arabs so?"

"What do you mean?"

"Well, once I heard him call the Arabs vicious mean animals. For Conn, 'bastard' usually sufficed."

"I don't understand."

"Well, he must have seen some Arab atrocity that really rankled. You know he had been around."

Deborah searched the past and her face was a jewel of concentration. "No, no. Not near our village. As you know we were in the South and the only danger was from Egyptian regulars. And they were all right. No. Conn never dealt with anyone but the Arabs in our village. And they are fine people. Some, I am sorry to say, left at the time."

"Sorry?"

"Certainly. We wanted to build a country, not create a refugee problem. As you know we had 2,000 years as

134

refugees. Some left because they thought we would lose and they did not want to be there when we did. Others thought they could return and get back their own homes plus ours. And some were frightened of us. But we never drove them out. Never. Especially our village. And of course some stayed. Like the vice president of the Knesset. He is an Arab. Did you know that?"

"No, I didn't."

"Remo, that tells me something about you."

"What does it tell you?"

"Some of the things you're not."

Remo accepted the statement and made no comment on it. Deborah switched the subject. "I can't think of any atrocity he would have seen."

"He was vehement, Debby. Can I call you Debby?"

"No. Deborah. What would make him vehement?" Suddenly she clasped a hand to her mouth. She shook her head, but there was laughter in her eyes. "Oh, that man, he is impossible. Impossible."

"What is it?"

"You know Conn MacCleary?"

"Yes."

"And I told you of the still?"

"Yes." Remo looked at Deborah quizzically. He was supposed to be able to figure something out and now he wanted to very much.

"Come on. You knew Conn. What were his exact words?"

Remo thought back, and if he had not tried so hard, he knew he would remember. "I can't remember exactly."

"Would degenerate scum animals refresh your memory?"

"Yes. That's right. That is what he called them."

135

"Well, then, what is the greatest atrocity on earth for Conn MacCleary?"

"The murder of children?"

"That's a tragedy, Remo. I'm talking about MacCleary. An atrocity."

"An atrocity? Degenerate scum animals?" He paused, then asked almost as a question, but it was not a question. He knew.

"They got his still?"

Deborah reached her hand to Remo's shoulder. "The Egyptian Air Force blasted it to smithereens. It was incredible. They saw the sandbags, I mean it was obvious from the air. The still had changed their colors and the damned thing glowed at night. They hit it with everything they had. Spitfires. The whole thing. But as you know, if you're bombing stills you're not bombing fortifications or towns. He must have saved the village. But the still was wiped out."

And both Deborah and Remo said in unison: "The degenerate scum animals."

"Remo, you should have seen him. That was all he talked about for days. Degenerate scum animals. He volunteered for the Negev front but he was not accepted. Then he left and I guess your conflict with the Russians started heating up. Espionage war. And he returned to your service. Where I am sure you met him."

"Hush, hush," Remo said.

"And I know now why you are here and I am not afraid. Friend." She extended her hand and Remo took it.

"Friend," he said. And he leaned forward and kissed her on the lips. And she kissed him.

Softly, she said, "Not tonight." Which can never really be said without hurting someone who wants you.

"Okay," Remo said, "not tonight."

136

"You will see me tomorrow?"

"I think I can make it."

"You're full of shit. You'll make it."

"Maybe," Remo said. And he reached an arm behind her back and pulled her to him standing up. They both stood and kept their lips together and Remo moved a hand to her blouse and then over a breast which he pressed with warmth.

"You bastard," she whispered. "I really did not want to tonight."

"Why?"

"Because I do not want it that way. Not you coming in and then . . . not that way. Tomorrow night."

"You do not want me?"

"I wanted you from the moment you said Conn's name. Your face then was beautiful. You showed goodness and I am so alone here. And for a moment we were not alone anymore."

"I almost got killed out in the circle, looking at you."

"You're a stupid man. Looks. Like every man. I'm just looks to you."

"You began as looks."

"Remo. I want you tonight. Very much. But please, I do not want you coming in and taking me. I do not want you thinking you can just walk in and take me."

"Was that what you were frightened of?"

"No. Of course not. I told you. Tomorrow night."

"I could take you now."

"Yes."

"And you would not like it?"

"I would love it. But please."

Suddenly the phone rang. It was a jarring, persistent ring and Remo reached to rip the cord out of the wall, but

Deborah got to the phone first and out of his arms. She played shield with the phone while she talked.

"Yes," she said. "Yes. Yes. Dammit. Are you sure? Does it have to be that way? Yes. I'm sorry. Yes, yes. Of course. Of course."

She hung up the phone and cocked her head. "There is nothing like a telephone to protect chastity. Tomorrow, Remo."

And Remo acquiesced like a gentleman. Gently he took the phone in the palm of his left hand and with an ungentlemanly right hand brought the palm edge down and through, cracking the receiver and the carriage. Then he split the fucking insides in a screeching gaggle of colored wires.

"Tomorrow," he said sweetly and dropped the two halves of the great American technology on the floor.

Deborah smiled. "Oh, you big frightening man. You're so terrifying." And she went to him and kissed him and tugged him, like a little boy to the door. "Oh, you're such a terror. Cracking telephones and beating up mororcycle people. Oh, you're so terrible." She gave him a playful punch in the stomach, kissed him with finality on the lips, spun him around out the door, where the insects were still trying to gather a quorum, and shut the door, disposing of the most perfect human weapon in a nation's arsenal like a little toy top.

And Remo loved it. He told himself he would not think about the first time he had really met MacCleary, who had posed as a priest in Remo's death cell and offered the pill of life on the end of a cross, MacCleary, who had engineered his supposed death only to bring him to what the world thought was a sanitarium to begin training that would never end, MacCleary who had made the incredi-

138

bly stupid mistake of becoming vulnerable, MacCleary, who being vulnerable, had to be killed.

MacCleary. Remo Williams' first assignment and the only one he was unable to complete. MacCleary who had wound up doing Remo's job by using his hooked arm to rip tubings from his own throat in a hospital bed. MacCleary, the stupid bastard who believed that it was right to die for a tomorrow where his type would not be needed. MacCleary, who by his death, had sealed Remo Williams into his new life just as surely as if the bandages covering his fatal wounds now bound Remo.

Remo Williams who had not missed an assignment since. Remo Williams. Who if Dial-a-Prayer in Chicago should have said something from Deuteronomy that noon, would have visited that night with Deborah, taken her on a quiet walk. And killed her.

But the good Reverend had not read from Deuteronomy and Smith had given him a day off, a day from peak. And it was the good warm August of Virginia. He would spend tomorrow with Deborah, and he would make a beautiful day. It was more than many people had.

But then Dr. Nils Brewster found the body of Dr. James Ratchett.

CHAPTER NINETEEN

Dr. James Ratchett had always imagined his death would be a dramatic affair.

In his youth, he had visions of stark white hospital beds where he forgave people. Dying, he forgave his parents, then his sister. Sometimes he would fantasize dying with a curse, ripping out the tubing from his swollen arm and refusing life.

His mother would promptly slash her wrists, his sister would carry an indelible wound for life. And his father? Damn his father. Even in fantasies, he could not imagine his father being very interested in anything James did. Even in fantasy, his father would be telephoned at his Wall Street office, the message taken by his trim, attractive secretary. She would tell him at 6:30 that night over cocktails, before retiring to their apartment.

"Ripped it out of his arm, you say?," his father would ask. "Cursed me on his death bed? Hmmm. Never knew little James had it in him."

James was nine when he had these fantasies. When he

was fourteen, he had different fantasies. It was his father in a hospital bed, and James was ripping the tubing from his father's arm, because he had just realized what a filthy, hairy, grotesque pig he was.

At fourteen, James had made concoctions. He would give them to friends. He once gave a concoction to a neighbor's boy, five years younger than he. The boy was in a coma for three days and James was sent where people made sure you didn't brew poisons for younger boys to drink.

They sent him to the Bilsey School, Dorchester, England, where proper young English gentlemen went through a homosexual phase. For James, it was not a phase. Denied chemical equipment and chemicals, he devoted himself to theorizing about them. He continued this at Rensselaer Polytechnic Institute in upstate New York where he had all the equipment he needed, but remained addicted to theory, it being so much cleaner and neater.

He received a science degree from Harvard and a doctorate in theoretical chemistry from M.I.T. His senior thesis won him international fame and his evening activities earned him three suspended sentences for contributing to the delinquency of minors. To get the last two sentences suspended was extremely expensive, exhausting his inheritance. This meant he could not continue toward his doctorate in mathematics. He would have to teach. Teaching meant constantly dealing with people, perhaps as much as five hours a week.

Then came Brewster Forum. He could design his own cottage. Of course, Dr. Brewster understood how people's tastes varied and why not be sensible? And Dr. James Ratchett found a home, and sometimes even an audience for his hypnotism which he had learned as a child under the mistaken impression that it would guarantee him endless lovers.

But the hypnotism of the night before had left a malignant, gnawing remembrance of something just about to be remembered, but reluctant to come forward. It was a cry of ready or not, here I come, and then nothing came.

So. He would wrestle it away from his memory. To do so, one must be prepared. You do not grab a thought like a little boy's neck. You tease it, coax it. Ignore it. You make yourself very comfortable without it and then it jumps forward to join the party.

Dr. James Ratchett undressed and left his clothes outside his very special room. It was a masterpiece of engineering, that room, a white bowl shape, upholstered all around with white vinyl, over a layer of water that cushioned the floors and the rounded walls as high up as a man could reach. Ratchett's acquaintances called it his womb-room but he thought of it as his den.

Into the room, he had brought his pipe with a sliver of hashish. The pipe lit when he pressed a button, and Ratchett brought the smoke deep down into his lungs and held his breath. He became aware of his limbs: how distant they were and how he was holding his breath. He was holding his breath forever and his head felt nothing. Nothing was what he felt in his head and he just let the air out because he felt like it. But he didn't have to. He could have held the air in for hours. Yes. And deep in again. My, so cool it was. He listened to the coolness of the room and felt the vinyl on the ceiling with his eyes and suddenly his white womb was very funny. Here he was in a water mish-mesh.

"Mish-mesh," he said and laughed hysterically. "Mishmesh," he said again, wishing he had someone in the room who could appreciate the humor of the joke.

142

And the vinyl covered door opened. And that was a woman. Yes. Really a woman. Perhaps she had come for a drag. Perhaps he would offer her some. But he would not talk to her at all. No talking.

Oh, she was undressed too, and she carried a whip and where he had a thing, she just had a brownish-blond blotch. He would show her. He would not get an erection. He never could. But then she was doing something and he had something. And then he took another drag, and then. . . . Cut. A scream. Rip.

Dr. James Ratchett grabbed at his stinging numb groin and nothing was there but warm wet blood, gushing wet blood, splattering around him on the white vinyl, making standing slippery, and he fell, and grabbed desperately looking for something to stop the blood.

"Oooh, oooh," the cries came out of his lungs, as he slithered around his room, toward the door. Reach it. Out. Help. But it was locked, and Dr. James Ratchett slid back toward the center of the room and found he could not even bite his way out, as he chewed into the vinyl harder and harder, and then his teeth tore a hole in the vinyl, and water spilled in, mixing with his blood, and he sloshed around in the pink puddle, in the agony of red death.

And then he remembered where he saw her and who had taken the pictures and why she had now killed him.

CHAPTER TWENTY

Nils Brewster was in a sweat. His tumbleweed hair was matted with moisture. His arms flailed and his mouth moved violently as it shrieked out sounds at Remo. He had stopped Remo on the gravel driveway near Deborah's cottage just as the sun moved overhead into noon. It was Remo's day off peak.

"Oooh. Oooh. Oho," said the world's foremost authority on the dynamics of hostility, the man who had written what many considered to be the definitive work on mass murder. "Uh ... uh ... uh," he added, and then collapsed at Remo's feet.

It was panic all right. Remo knelt down and let Brewster recover. There was no danger of shock.

Soon Brewster opened his eyes. "Ratchett. Oooh. Ahhh. Oho."

It would be no use to tell Brewster to calm down. Only idiots offered that sort of advice to panicky people. To tell someone to calm down when he was panicked was to tell him that you were not aware of the seriousness of the situation. That the situation could not be improved by panic was of little import. The person had something so awesome to convey that he was unable to convey it. To keep your head while he lost his only let him know that he was not getting through to you, and made him try even harder with less success.

So Remo did what he knew was right, even though he did not wish Deborah to see it from her window if she was standing there.

He repeated Brewster's desperate yell. "Ooooh. Ahhhh. Oho," he shouted, looking directly into Brewster's eyes.

Remo joined Brewster in his hysteria, in order to bring Brewster back with him to coherency.

"Ratchett," Remo gasped.

"Ratchett," Brewster gasped. "Dead."

"Ratchett is dead," Remo moaned.

"Ratchett murdered. Blood."

"Ratchett has been murdered. There's lots of blood."

And Brewster nodded and said: "I went to his place just now. His special place. He was dead. Blood and water. He was dead. You."

"Me."

"Yes. Do something."

"Good. I'll do something."

"Walls. Fences. Machine guns. Help us."

"Yes, yes. Of course. Help you. Machine guns. Fences. Walls."

"Yes. Get the killers. Get them. Kill them. Destroy them. Bomb them."

"Yes."

"But don't let the police know."

"No, no. Of course not."

"Good," said Nils Brewster. His eyes wide, he rose to his feet. "We'll go now."

145

He was still unsteady as they crossed the small bridge over the brook and Remo gently guided him by applying light pressure to an elbow.

"Is that his house?," Remo asked, looking at the large white egg with windows.

Brewster nodded. "I didn't see him this morning. We had a 9 o'clock appointment and he's always punctual. I just wanted to explain to him that I thought his hypnotism had gone far enough and that we should look for some other form of his artistic expression. But he didn't show up, and he didn't answer the phone. So I came here. He has a special room, an obvious imitation of his concept of womb. And he was there, and the door was jammed from the outside."

The sun played over the house, as they approached it, as if boiling it for an egg salad lunch.

"I like it," Remo said.

"Nobody likes it."

"I like it. I think it's a hell of an idea for a home."

"It's grotesque," Brewster said.

"That's your opinion."

"That's the opinion of everyone in Brewster Forum."

"No, it's not."

"No? Who likes it?"

"I like it."

"Oh, you. Well, I'm talking about everyone."

"I'm someone."

"You're our security officer."

"But I'm a someone."

"Yes. All right. If you want to look at it that way. He's in there. I touched nothing." Brewster stood at the entrance. The door was ajar.

Remo nodded. "It's really hard to refrain from panic in a situation like this," Brewster said. "You may not have

146

noticed, but I was on the verge of panic. Fortunately, I have incredible self-control. But this pushed me to my limit."

"Okay," Remo said softly. Like most panic victims, Brewster had no recollection of his actions. He would not even remember fainting. "Stay here, Nils."

"Call me Dr. Brewster." He leaned against the door frame, still shaking. "We'd be in an awful fix if I were the type to lose my head," he said.

"Yes, Dr. Brewster, we would," Remo said.

"Call me Nils," Brewster said. Remo smiled reassuringly and went into the living room. He spotted the fireplace opening to Ratchett's special retreat. There was Ratchett, nude, his body half covered in a pink puddle of water and blood. His face was a final set mask of horror. Remo reached in, careful not to slosh around in the liquid, and flipped Ratchett over. So much for how they did it. Now they had attacked the scientists, and to save them it might be necessary to kill them. If he called the police now, the next passage from Dial-a-Prayer might well be Deuteronomy. Remo stepped back carefully and picked up Ratchett's phone. It was a vulnerable phone. But he was not doing business.

He dialed information, got the number of Dr. Deborah Hirshbloom, and dialed it. The phone rang. And rang. And rang. Remo looked to the ceiling without seeing, looked to the floor without seeing and whistled impatiently. And the phone rang.

"Shit," he said and hung up.

He went outside.

"Shocking, wasn't it?" said Brewster.

"What?" said Remo, his mind still on the phone call.

"You look upset."

"Oh. Yes. Shocking scene. Awful."

147

"If you were as familiar with violence and its dynamics as a human form of expression, if you were as familiar with it as I am, it might have been easier for you, son."

"I suppose so," Remo said. Dammit, she wasn't home. This was his day off peak. And he planned to spend it with her. All day and all night. And now she wasn't home.

Dr. Brewster reached for something in his pocket, and brought out a pipe and a ripped bag of tobacco. "How the hell did this happen?" he said, looking at the ripped pouch as if it had betrayed him. "My pants are dirty too. I must have brushed against something." He lit his pipe.

"Violence is a strange thing," Dr. Brewster said, musing on the smoke. "Many people never learn to accept it as a part of life."

She was supposed to be home. All right, maybe she had just gone out for something. Maybe she was just being funny. Playing a game. Or maybe she had changed her mind. The bitch. The little Israeli bitch had changed her mind.

The two men went back to the forum center, the scientist talking, musing, explaining, ponitficating, placing the elements of life and death in intellectual perspective. Remo Williams was planning. If she was just trying to make him wait, he would be very casual. Say that he wasn't sure of the time. Was she late? Oh. Or maybe he'd disappear for a while and be late himself. No. He'd see her and tell her she was immature.

"You see," Brewster explained. "Even though you are a policeman, you have not fully accepted the fact of violence as an integral part of man's life. You have not come to terms with the very obvious fact that man is a killer. And his greatest game is man himself. A predator. Only late in development did he become herbivorous. The

148

overreaction against violence in more backward American communities is an eruption of the sublimation of violence. Which is really not sick. Violence is healthy, human. Vital."

Maybe he would call her a kike and just walk away. But what if she laughed when he said that? Worse, what if she were hurt? He would apologize and hold her. But if she were really hurt, she wouldn't let him. No. Not Deborah. She would laugh. Right at him. In his face. Then he would laugh. Then it would be all right.

"I know it's difficult, son, but as I was explaining to some general or other, no, a congressman, I believe—well, in any case, one of those things. I told him that perhaps policemen like yourself are the ones who are least able to handle violence and therefore are drawn toward it as a profession. You know that's how we get funding?"

"What?" said Remo.

"How we get funding, son," Dr. Brewster explained. "You exploit their little dreams or fears. Whatever."

"What are you talking about?" Remo asked. He would take care of Deborah later. "I was finding it hard to follow."

"Our funding, son. The way to get funding is to decide what you want, then throw in something the government may want. As an afterthought. Like our study on the community life of combat."

"Yes?"

"Well, that paid for Schulter's animal experiments and Boyle's ethnic studies."

"I see," said Remo. "And your little plan to conquer the world?" He dropped the reference casually.

"That bought the golf course, the auditorium and about five more years of just about anything we want. I don't know why I trust you like this. I just do. I'm a good judge of men."

He was, thought Remo, like most people who do not work at it, a very bad judge of himself. He trusted now because he felt safe. Apparently, he had taken Remo's preoccupation with Deborah as shock over the Ratchett killing and no longer felt threatened by someone who might possibly be above panic.

"Is there a plan to conquer the world?"

"Yes, of course. You could conquer the world with 50,000 men. Provided, the rest of the world wanted to be conquered. Hah. You see, it takes the cooperation of the losers. But we're not going to include that in any study for at least three years though, not until we have another funding source. Your job is safe with us for another three years."

So it was just a hustle, after all. All the federal funds, the secrecy, the work of CURE, the deaths of McCarthy and Hawkins and Ratchett, all of it was only to allow these harmless nits to go on figuring up days and down days, drugging rhinoceroses and lowering heartbeats. A goddam hustle.

"I imagine Deborah was working on that plan."

"Don't call her Deborah. She's Dr. Hirshbloom. I personally don't mind, but you know how some of these medical doctors get. No, as a matter of fact, she wasn't the least bit interested. Recently, I've been getting the impression she is interested in nothing but chess. A fine mind. But very unproductive, I'm afraid."

"Uh, uh," said Remo, who noticed suddenly that he had been walking in his old manner, the natural walk of his youth and early manhood. His peak was falling rapidly now. Several times a day now, he was forced to go back mentally to his little room, where Chiun waited. But the effect was wearing off more and more rapidly. His vitality was ebbing.

Brewster was rambling on about his plan to conquer the world. Of course, it could be pulled off if each soldier in the Army could be brought up to twenty percent capacity. Did it shock Remo that the average man used less than ten per cent? But no one yet, Brewster said, had reached twenty per cent. He wasn't even sure if a human being could survive using twenty per cent of his capabilities. So, in a way, the forum was really giving the government its money's worth. A brilliant plan that was impossible. Generals like those sort of things.

Remo tried to concentrate on the room, but the sidewalk still thumped hard against his heels. He pulled oxygen deep into his groin, but still felt winded. He thought of Deborah and for a moment was exhilirated. He realized. She was uninterested in the work of Brewster Forum because she did not come to work for Brewster Forum.

She was an agent, all right. Her control proved that, even when she was afraid of him. And she was beginning to fall in love with him. The alienation of their lives had been broken and both shared the first flushes of knowing someone. That was why things had moved so well the night before.

And Conn MacCleary was the key. The Israelis wouldn't let Conn fight his holy war against the Arabs after they had desecrated the sanctity of his still because, quite simply, Conn MacCleary was not in Israel to fight Arabs or even to train people to fight Arabs.

Conn MacCleary, master of the personal attack, was training people to seek a different enemy. And it would also explain why he volunteered and why Deborah had not listed the real name of her village, and why, if it was so secret, the presence of Arabs would in no way compromise it.

This little village was the first training ground for the agents who would follow those who had processed people in ovens, stripped human flesh for lampshades, tore off genitals with pliers, experimented on babies and women and men to see how long it took shock to set in when an organ was ripped off or when you tied a woman's legs together during labor. The village was a training site for people to track down Nazis and Deborah was on the trail of one.

And that one must be the killer, the one who had brought about the deaths of McCarthy and Now Ratchett. Because they had somehow gotten in the way of his plan to get the compromising photos of the Forum's staff. But why did he want the pictures? Probably to blackmail the staff into giving him the little plan to conquer the world. Well, the joke was on him. The plan to conquer the world was a hoax, only Brewster's way of getting more federal funds.

Remo would have a good day off peak. And if Deborah asked him to, he would help set up a snatch or a kill on the one she was after. He would show her how good he was. And then they would make love.

"You know," Remo said to Dr. Brewster, "it's a beautiful day." They were at the phone booth on the corner. I'll be right out."

"You're not going to phone the police or something. I mean, what are you going to do?"

"I'll take care of it," Remo said assuringly.

"You're sure you're all right now? You were pretty shocked before, son. And I wouldn't want you to do anything that would embarrass you or anything. Not many people can accept the violence we saw today, and I want you to know that I don't hold it against you."

"Thank you," said Remo. "But I think I can handle it."

Brewster put a fatherly hand on Remo's arm. "I'm sure you can, son. I'm sure you can. And if the police need more information, I'll be right here."

"Oh, I think I've got most of the information they need," Remo said. "Somebody cut off Dr. Ratchett's penis and he died from shock caused by loss of blood, while flailing around in a pink puddle of gore. They'll find out for sure when they take his lungs out in the autopsy."

Dr. Nils Brewster nodded sagely and collapsed on the gravel before the booth in a dead faint. Remo removed the pipe from where it had fallen near Brewster's head. It was still lit and could have set the tumbleweed hair afire.

And that afternoon, the good Reverend gave Remo some delightful news. He was not only off peak, but he was to leave. Immediately. Remo spoke the number into the tape recording and waited. Dr. Brewster was blissfully in the land of out.

A car passed and the driver offered to help. It was Anna Stohrs, the blonde with the hard face. Remo waved her away, angrily, and with a hard glint in her eyes she gunned the gas pedal and sped off.

Remo whistled softly to himself as he kept the cradle down with his elbow. Some day he might set the record for holding down a receiver without moving. Guinness Book of Records: Remo Williams, three hours and fifty-two minutes. Let's hear it for clean living and expensive training. But how could somebody pose people in sex photos without their knowing? Hypnotism? Too hard. Too hard. It must be drugs.

The bing of the first ring and Remo released the cradle.

"What is it now?" Smith sounded angry. That meant he was happy.

"I'd like to stay a day. Here."

"No."

"I've got something I'm working on."

"No," said Smith. "Just do what you're supposed to do."

"One of the people here has met with an accident."

"That's all right. Doesn't matter."

"I know about the little plan."

"Forget it."

"Aren't you interested?"

"If I see you in a year or so, you can tell me all about it."

"Well, why the sudden go?"

There was silence. And then Smith said in a calm but pained voice: "You're asking me a why?"

"I'm sorry. I really am."

"So am I. I'll attribute it to the inordinately long peak."

"Well, screw you," Remo said. "You ding-dongs set the peak, not me."

"Look. Rest."

"I'm not getting off till I get the reason. I want to stay another day."

"If you must know, another agency had moved into it. Remember the paint shop? Well, it's become an international, and they're working with an ally. In twenty-four hours that place is going to be crawling with agents. We're not needed now. So if you suddenly feel some need to perform some public service that is not your job, why don't you help with the garbage collection?"

"I want that extra day."

"Why?" Smith was getting annoyed.

"Would it surprise you if I told you I want to get laid." Remo used hard terms, lest Smith suspect affection.

"Anyone special?"

154

"One of the scientists."

"Not that fairy?"

"No. Doctor Hirshbloom."

"Remo." Smith's voice was suddenly harsh and imperious. "Stay away from her. She's an ally and she'll be working with our people to clear up this mess. She'll finger the targets."

"She'll work better if she's well-laid."

"Leave her alone."

"What about the sex photographer?"

"All part of the same thing. Blackmail against the government. I tell you, it's in good hands. Now get out of there before you get arrested for loitering. We're closing this number. We'll reach you. You get lost until we do. That's an order."

Remo hung up. Screw Smith and screw CURE. He was staying and he was having his day with Deborah. That was it. Insubordination. He had peaked too long. If he hung around, they would be after him to set him up. But a setup is not a follow-through and he was not a part to be replaced easily. Or was he?

Well, if it came to that, he couldn't think of a better reason to go. Conrad MacCleary chose patriotism. Remo Williams chose a woman. Maybe another day, he would feel differently. But today was today and it was August and he was going to stick it to Deborah, and then go to Henrici's Restaurant in Dayton, Ohio, for a Wednesday night meal, and keep going to Wednesday night meals until they found him.

On impulse, he dialed Dial-a-Prayer again. A tape recording told him "The number you have reached is not a working number."

Fast.

Outside, Brewster was coming to. The first words he

155

said to Remo as soon as he regained his balance were "Are you all right, son?"

"Yes, Nils. Thank you."

"Do you need help?"

"I . . . ." Remo paused. "Couldn't make the phone call to the police."

"That's all right. I understand. You've been through hell. It's a very difficult job to be security officer."

"I don't know if I can, can continue in the job. Not now."

"Yes, you can," Brewster said firmly. "Because we're doubling your salary. You're the first policeman good enough for the job. And that's that. Don't say no. I know men. You're the first one good enough for Brewster Forum. I'll make the phone call to the police."

Remo thanked Dr. Brewster who fumbled a dime into the telephone and dialed the emergency number listed on the board above the coin slots. He winked at Remo, made an okay sign with his right hand, and began to babble incoherently into the receiver.

Remo waved at Brewster, who was gesticulating wildly with his free hand, as he shouted into the phone: "Dead. Aaah. Dead. Ooooh. Help. Dead. Brewster Forum. Blood."

And Remo sauntered off, flatfooted, off balance and laughing at himself. The flush of relaxation might have explained why he was about to enter the first black-out period of his life.

156

The man once known as Dr. Hans Frichtmann examined the new negatives. The lighting was not as good as on the others, but it would do. And the set was complete. He would take pains that no illiterate cop would steal these as McCarthy must have done with the first set. An insignificant Irish life for a brilliant plan. Funny how a flea could clog a great engine.

"Well, no matter. The Jewess had been the last. One could almost develop a fondness for the animals if they were not so annoying.

The average German had not understood. They had reaped the benefits, but they did not want to know about the dirty work. They had almost made the world Jew-free, and did the world appreciate it? How did they expect them to get rid of Jews if not by gassing them and burning them?

Oh, certainly everyone at home cheered when you were on top and they did not have to get their sweet little hands dirty. But when you lost, the shock. No one was political.

157

Not when you lost. But they had cheered you when you were winning. Did they expect the Jews to disappear without mass killing? Just by wishing? Of course, it was unpleasant. That was the price one must pay. There were even some Jews he would have saved if he could. Some he respected more than Germans. But if you started making an exception here and an exception there, then where were you? Jews. All over.

He didn't ask for the Jews to be in the world. He hadn't put them there. Hadn't made them like they were. He was building a better world. And if it took some unpleasantness, then certain brave people would do it. Nobody had seen the Germany he had seen or lived in the Germany he had lived in. Chaos. Disorder. Der Fuhrer had ended it and given Germany back its soul.

But the Germans had failed the party and the nation. Because they were not worthy of their heritage. A little trouble and they collapsed, and then every one of the little hypocrites ran around saying he didn't know, he was sorry. Well, they were not strong enough to know, only to reap the benefits. They could have known. The evidence was there.

Where did they think all the Jews went that disappeared in box cars? To Grossinger's?

He had to laugh at that. Even the generals in their cars and with their fancy servants. Turning their heads, going through convulsions not to see the blood that he had to live through daily. And he was a doctor. But he was a German and a Nazi.

Their clean hands. The swine. Looking down on him. How dare they, those generals? He remembered a night at Horcher's in Berlin. It had been furlough from the camp in Poland. He had sent a drink to the young staff officer,

158

sitting with his lady friend at the next table. The drink had come back untouched.

"What? An officer from the Afrika Corps refusing a drink? I've never heard of such a thing."

He said this with as much warmth as possible. They were all Germans after all, especially under the new order. He had gone through medical school, the son of a carpenter. So the officer obviously was aristocracy. But what did that mean now? In the new Germany, they were all one. One race. The master race.

"Will you not share a drink with a fellow officer?" he had asked. And the arrogant swine had answered:

"With a fellow officer I would."

That had done it. "You think you are so fine in here, eating the best of foods, drinking the best of wines. Why do you live so well? Because of me."

The officer had tried to ignore him. But one could not ignore a man who refused to be ignored.

"I see your lady friend eats delicately. In our camps we do not have the luxury of delicacy. We must have the gold teeth pulled out of the heads of Jews because Germany needs the money. To pay you and put wine on your table. The fatherland needs the hair of Jew children and the clothes of the processed people.

"Who do you think is putting the food on that table? I am. By killing the inferior races so that you can live in your delicate comfort. Do you know what it is like to rip out someone's testicles? But I must, so we will know more about reproduction for your comfort.

"Hey, high-class lady! Have you ever seen so many people in a ditch, that the blood seeps up through the earth that covers it? Does that go well with your chocolate mousse? Eh? How does that go?"

They had left, of course. Run away, leaving the dirty

159

work for men strong enough to do it. Naturally, he had been arrested that night for disorderly conduct and given a stern rebuke for his loose tongue. But doctors were scarce. And the SS understood, despite what was said of them after the war.

He put the negatives back in the envelope. With these, he had just the wedge to give his new employers who, as coincidence would have it, were also building a great new world. With these, one could easily begin to work effectively. Oh, not to get anything major all at once, but to force a scientist to take a visit to a city in another country and just talk about things. These photos could enslave America's greatest brains for their entire lifetimes.

A perfect plan. Almost ruined by that Irish cop, but salvaged. The new policeman? Well, he was something more. Luckier than McCarthy and better. But still only a policeman and it was too late for him to do anything anyway. Dr. Hans Frichtmann allowed himself a touch of regret that he would not be around long enough to teach a final permanent lesson to Remo Pelham.

CHAPTER TWENTY-TWO

First there was the note.

Deborah was not home. The door was unlocked, her cottage empty of her, and a note on the desk, sealed in an envelope with Remo's name on it. The bitch. The little Jew bitch. That little whore Remo had been willing to die for, just to screw. She probably gave it away for shekels.

Smith had been right. He had been descending so fast that he was incapable of correct judgment. She had given him a feel and sidestepped him. Quick and neat.

Well, he would find her. He would find Miss Quick and Neat and break her arm. Just to let you know, baby, you ain't that good. No. Never mind. He would read the note and leave. And if he ever saw her again, he would kill her, because she would recognize him.

He ripped open the envelope, not bothering to turn on the light but reading from the late afternoon sun coming vaguely through the windows.

"Darling Remo."

Oh, what a little bullshitter she was. Cunt.

"I never told you why I especially loved Conn Mac-
Cleary."

Because he screwed you when you were three.

"I was an ugly child, with many freckles. Youngsters as
you know can be cruel."

As opposed to women.

"The other children tormented me because of my freckles. My nickname was the Hebrew children's equivalent of
shit-face."

Even then they knew.

"One day, Conn heard the remark. And he looked
surprised. 'Do you know,' he said, 'that a woman without
freckles is like a night without stars?' And of course the
other children said, but what about a girl? And he told
them that a girl with freckles is like the dawn of life, the
beauty of a new day, and she is so beautiful that like the
shining sun, some people could not see the beauty right
away. I guess that started it. I just always believed I
would be beautiful and there is nothing like that to en-
courage the reality of it. That started my swelled head, of
course. Conn probably had a bag on, I don't remember. But
that sort of talk is easy to take. In any case, Remo, I grew
up in a house where every so often my father would leave.
And although they did not want that life for me, I followed
it. I guess I had to follow it. Maybe I wanted to follow it.
You see enough numbers tattooed on people's arms and
hear enough stories and you know what you must do.

"That is what has brought me here. One of *them*. Have
you ever heard of Hans Frichtmann? The butcher of
Treblinka? Here at the Forum.

"I should not tell you this, but it is of no matter. I have
already made so many mistakes since meeting you, telling
you this in print probably will not matter. I love you,
Remo. And if I saw you again, I would be hopelessly in

162

love. And because you are who you are and I am who I am, this could not be. Maybe I am deluding myself into believing that you were not deluding me. If you were, I salute you. But this delusion, then, of your love, I will cherish until the last long night without stars.

"I guess all of us carry our histories like crosses and our destinies like fools. But occasionally, we must succumb to logic. And the logic of our situation is that our love would destroy us. If we could only shake our duties like old dust. But we cannot. Mad dogs yet roam the world and for those we love, we must search them out, fighting all the time to keep our humanity despite the pressures to fight dogs like dogs.

"We gave each other only an hour and a promise. Let us cherish that hour in the small places which keep us kind. You are kind and good and really very gentle. Do not let your enemies ever destroy that, darling. For as surely as the Jordan flows, we shall, if we maintain that goodness, meet again in that morning that never ends. This is our promise that we will keep. I love you, Remo.

"Deborah."

Well, shit. That's a woman for you. Of course, she loved him. How else could she call him kind and good and gentle? The utter silliness of it all. Remo read the letter again and felt very good. Then he tore it up, because precautions were precautions, and lit the pieces with a match.

She was obviously finishing her assignment, and Remo would, as he painfully knew, only be in the way of it. So the simple thing was to go to Dayton, and then buy a ticket to Chicago, and there find someone who vaguely looks like you and who has a passport. Then kindly, good and gentle Remo Williams would work something on the poor bastard, and be out of the country and headed toward Israel and that town in the Negev.

163

He would go there, find her parents, and wait. He would tell her parents to mention some phrase from the note. And she would come running home. CURE would find him though. Well, he'd work something out. All this think and counterthink had been a bother anyway. Hell, maybe he'd just find her now and they would both go somewhere.

Remo watched the last scrap of paper burn and, leaving the cottage, accidentally bumped into the door. To hell with it. Everyone bumped into doors.

He was tired now, very tired. The sun drained him and the walking drained him. He stumbled on the walk. He had pressed too hard too long and now he was running down. He was sweating now, for real. Real sweat from the afternoon heat. He stumbled again.

He looked up and saw Brewster's office. He would rest there awhile and then leave. Stephanie was at the door, but he didn't feel like talking. He tried to pat her on the head. But inexplicably his hand missed and he fell full-length on the polar bear rug. He crawled to the couch, and pulled himself up onto it. In the cool of the air conditioning, he drifted off. Out.

Then there was the sleep. It was a deep, unconscious leaving. And there were dreams.

Chiun, his aged Korean instructor, saying: "Do not pass this point. Do not pass this point. Do not pass this point."

And other voices, Oriental voices. And Chiun was telling the other voices that he had not passed the point yet, so they must stand back. And Chiun wore black robes and a black headband and he was motioning that Remo should go to his special room and stay there. He should stay there until everything was all right. Chiun would sit with him. Remo had just worked too hard and too long.

Remo should go into the room and Chiun would sit with him and talk to him.

And since he wasn't doing anything important at the moment other than dying, Remo decided to go into the room where Chiun was waiting. He could always die. That was Chiun talking. Funny, he thought he had been saying that. But it was Chiun saying that. Remo could die later if he wished. He could die any time he wanted. Promise? Yes. Chiun promised.

So Remo went. It was very cold in the room and Chiun looked very mean and stern. He was not here to punish Remo but to save him. But you promised I could die?

You cannot die.

I want to die.

You may not. There are things you must do because your life is precious.

Leave me alone. I want to die. You promised.

But you are in the room now, Remo, and here you are not permitted to die.

You're a liar.

Yes, I lied to you. I hurt you.

Yes, you do.

I will hurt you more. For I am in this room with you and I am going to hurt you more. You will feel great pain.

I do not want to hurt.

Listen. You are dying. But I will not let you die, Remo. I prepared this room so that you should not die. That is why together we prepared this room. Your room, Remo. It holds your youth. Without the miracle of rest, you have lived a lifetime in three months. You are an old man, Remo. All that you took by your will and your effort has been taken back because you used it too long. But watch. We will do a trick. Come with me and do the trick. See the fire. It is hot. Hot. We will run through the

165

fire. The trick is the fire. Come. Yes, it hurts, but come. I will go with you. Now. Into the fire.

And he was roasting alive, in incredible, flashing pain, that seared his flesh. The flames burned his feet and licked at his legs, then engulfed his entire body in a whooshing roar.

And Remo Williams was standing, yelling in the air-conditioned office and little Stephanie Brewster was terrified beside him. The room smelled faintly of jasmine and the chill made Remo shake. Was it his imagination, the residue of the dream, or did he smell burning flesh?

Remo rubbed his forehead, and felt something crumble over his eyes. It was charred hair on his eyebrows, curled white ashes that powdered in his fingers.

Stephanie lost her terror and began clapping. "Oh, do that again. Do it again. Wonderful."

"What?," asked Remo.

"I didn't know you did magic."

"What magic?"

"You just lay down and shut your eyes and then you lit up almost like a light bulb. Oh, it was stellar. Stellar. Very unusual. That's redundant. Something isn't very unusual. It's unusual."

"How long was I here?"

"Well, I didn't have my stop watch. But I would guess two or three minutes. You looked very tired when you came in, and then you fell, and your hands were cold, and I thought you were having a coronary. But I didn't know you did magic."

"Yeah, kid. That's the biz. Look. I'm late for an appointment. Tell your dad that I'm going on vacation and I may not be back because the forum is too rough for me. Okay?"

"I'll write it down," said Stephanie. With her awkward six-year-old hands, she maneuvered a pencil over several pieces of note paper, in a handwriting reminiscent of someone designing a rope.

"I paraphrased," she explained, starting on the first page which contained half a word. "Feelings of inadequacy impel Remo Pelham's resignation."

"You've got it, sweets."

"Well?"

"Well, what?"

"Aren't you going to kiss me goodbye?" And Remo Williams kissed Stephanie Brewster goodbye and she crinkled her nose, explaining that his face was hot.

"That's the biz, kid," Remo said with lightness of heart, and he left with his very dry clothes crackling around him toward his appointment in Dayton. Wait in Israel for an agent to come home? Remo chuckled. He never would have made it out of Chicago. Well, senility is senility.

His body hurt, like a very bad sunburn, but it was a good hurt. He was breathing well and moving well and relaxed and alive. He wished Deborah all the best and assumed she would be well because, after all, she was very lucky. She would have died on Deuteronomy. That's the biz.

Still, he felt a little desire to read the note again, just once more. But it had gone up in flames and just as well. He would relax, go out of his head in Dayton, fornicate a bit, and maybe start slow in a week or two. Perhaps they would move Chiun out to him for one of the training programs. He would probably need that.

An ambulance moved toward him from the other side of the circle. It couldn't be Ratchett. His house was in the other direction.

Then there was the body.

The ambulance slowed and a patrolman riding in front called out: "You must be Pelham."

"Yes," said Remo.

167

"You're the security officer. You want to meet me at the morgue?"

"Well, I'm sort of busy," Remo said, and seeing the young policeman's face contort in shock, he felt somewhat stupid. "I'm clearing up some things here. I'll be with you later. I've had a hard day."

"So has she," said the patrolman, nodding back to the receiving section of the ambulance. "Another OD. Your second in a month. I thought you people up here were brains, not junkies. Look. You've got to make it to the morgue because we're checking out stuff with the FBI. Hey, what happened to your face?"

"I got too close to a stove."

"Oh. Just a second." And to the driver he said, "Wait a minute."

The policeman left the seat and sidled up to Remo and in confidential tones that the driver could not hear said, "Look, no matter what they say, the FBI goes out of its way to grab credit. You know what I'm talking about."

Remo nodded.

"They told us that if anyone saw you to tell you to meet them at the morgue. I know what they're doing. They want to get you away from the photographers over on the thirteenth green. That's where we found the body. Fuck 'em. You're the security officer. If you make it there fast, you can still get to see a reporter. Know what I mean. I mean they come in here to make a pinch or something that we can do just as good and they act so goddam nicey-nicey like they don't want the credit. Know what I mean?"

Remo understood.

"How does that make us look, right? And you. You're security officer. Both of us together don't make what those bastards make. Right? All we got is our respect. Right?"

Remo nodded. "I'd like to see the body."

"She's a shrink. Would you believe it? A shrink OD'ing on horse? What a bunch of dingalings. Hey, watch it with those stoves, fella. You look awful."

"The body."

"Sure. But she's wrapped."

"Just a look?"

"Sure. Hey, don't start up yet."

The driver shook his head. "Where do you think I'm rushing to, man?"

When they got to the rear, the patrolman confided that the driver's entire race was lazy. He opened the doors and with the effected cynicism of young policemen, said: "That's it."

Remo saw the sheet covering the being on the folding stretcher. He knew it was Deborah. He reached into the ambulance and carefully, very carefully, folded back the sheet, controling every nerve lest his hands break away. He could feel the tremble of energy course through him, and he channelled it into the precision he knew he needed, and he felt something rise in him, something trained and yet beyond training.

And he saw the still face and the closed eyes and the freckles which had lit his night of loneliness and the lips which were now still and the arms that would never move again. He reached in and held her hand. In the light from the overhead bulb he saw on her arm something that was being surrendered, either by the chemicals he knew were in her or by the life that was no longer in her. The faint blue rectangle which looked as though drawn by a robin's egg crayon. They had been neat little numbers once that the master race used to catalog the human beings they considered subhuman, even precious children who, for a brief

169

moment, would light up a life, and having lit it, could set in motion that which would settle an old, old score.

He squeezed her hand. It was hard, unyielding. Tenderly, he opened the fingers and removed the object that she clutched. He looked at it, then put in his shirt pocket. Deborah was supposed to lead our agents to the killer. Now, in death, she would lead Remo to the master race who thought they were supermen.

Well, then, he would let them know what one was. One who was not sure of where he had come from because he was left at a Catholic orphanage, one who, for all he knew, contained the seeds of all races. He might even be a pureblood German. If that should be, thought Remo, should they hold some special lien on viciousness, let that enjoy itself within him now. Chiun's ancient scripture flashed through his mind: "I am created Shiva, the destroyer; death, the shatterer of worlds." They would come to know the destroyer.

And then Remo covered the stars for the last time and could have sworn that he gently shut the ambulance doors. He had been very precise about it, doing it very slowly to appear casual.

But the bang and the crack of the door and the caved-in red cross, and the ambulance settling on its wheels brought the driver running from the cab. The patrolman yelled and Remo shrugged his shoulders.

"These fuckin' nuts they got here," the patrolman yelled to the driver, while he stared at Remo angrily. "They're all screwballs. Even the cop. What'd you do that for, huh?"

But he made no move toward Remo. And Remo again apologized, and walked away. He hoped he would arrive before the FBI. He had nothing against the FBI.

CHAPTER TWENTY-THREE

The man once known as Dr. Hans Frichtmann sat at his chessboard, staring at an endgame whose outcome was a foregone conclusion. Chess was a balm for the mind, the mind that could appreciate it.

He had donned his smoking jacket and wore slippers, befitting a man who had done a hard day's work. Who could have expected that the little Jewess worked for that vengeful gang that did not know World War Two was over? They were insane. And now that she was dead, another would be coming for him. But he would be gone. The pictures would enable the Russians to control the scientists at the Forum, and that had been his mission. He had done his job. Naturally, it would not be adequately appreciated, but appreciation was for the days as a young man.

He looked at the board again. Only a king left, against his black king, queen, two knights, a rook, and a bishop. But before the drug took effect the Jewess had said that no matter how bad things looked, there was a way. There was no way, of course.

He was about to reset the pieces for a new game when the door to his study was pushed open. It swung back on noiseless hinges, then the knob cracked into the wall.

It was the Brewster Forum security officer, looking as though he had climbed out of an oven.

"Hello, Stohrs," Remo said to the man who was Brewster's Forum's chess instructor. "I've come for my game."

"Well, not right now," Stohrs said.

"Oh, yes. Now is fine." He walked in and closed the door behind him.

"What do you want?," the chess instructor asked. "This is nonsense at such a late hour. You look terrible."

"I want to play chess."

"Well," said Stohrs with a sigh, "if you insist. Let me take your jacket."

Remo took it off himself and as he did, the frail fibers separated and a sleeve was torn. He noticed that his arms were red and swollen.

In the center of the room was the chess board on a metal stand on a bare parquet floor. Two heavy-armed oak chairs were attached to the table.

"Sit down, Mr. Pelham, I will set the board."

"No, this end game is fine. I will take white."

"You cannot win with only a king."

Remo reached into his shirt pocket and withdrew the white queen that Deborah's hand had surrendered to him in death. "I have a queen," he said. "That will be enough."

Remo rested his arms on the chair arms. Under his right forearm, he could feel the chill of metal conducting heat from his arm into the chair. He picked up his king to

172

examine the piece and as he did, looked down at the chair arm. He saw three small metal rings buried in the wood, with small holes, the diameter of needles, in the centers. That was it, Remo thought. A knockout injection.

Stohrs had taken his seat opposite Remo. "An interesting conclusion," he said. "It was reached through the Silician opening. Are you familiar with the Sicilian?"

"Yes, of course. He fought on the side of the Nazis. It was his responsibility to count the number of baby rapes committed by Hitler's thugs."

Remo smiled, and resisted the impulse to reach forward and to crush Stohr's adam's apple between his fingers. Time for that. Deborah had been here. She had sat in this chair, and looked in Stohrs' eyes, loathing him and what he stood for, but there because duty demanded it. She had lost the game. And then her life. The life was gone. But Remo could salvage the game. And he could give her life and her death at least that much meaning.

"Your move, Stohrs," Remo said, and Stohrs slid a pawn one space forward. "The pawns," he said. "The little men of the chess board. But they can become fighting pieces, the most dangerous in the game."

"Particularly when, like Nazis, they fight against women and children. They then are truly devastating."

Stohrs' face was red. He was about to speak when his daughter walked into the room. She wore a short red skirt and a white sweater with no bra. The darkening of her nipples was visible through the material. When she saw Remo, she licked her upper lip and her eyes took on a wild glint as if an interior light had flashed on, and pinpoints were shining through tiny openings in her eyeballs.

"Anna, we have an unexpected guest. Please prepare some refreshment."

173

"Of course, father," she said, and looked again at Remo. "What would you like?"

"Anything you have in the house will do. Baby's blood. Lampshade chips with cyanide dip. A heroin fizz. Whatever you're used to." Confusion painted her face with stupidity. Stohrs said, "Our guest is a very funny man. Just prepare the usual. And hurry."

"You seem, Mr. Pelham," Stohrs said after his daughter left, "to want to talk about Nazis."

"I have always been fascinated by insanity," Remo said.

"Our only insanity was that we lost."

"I'm glad to see that it's we," Remo said. "You lost because you wasted your energies attacking unnecessary targets. That's a sick toughness. The real toughness comes from Americans who don't go stoking ovens from hatred. That's why we win. The shits like you, the insane haters, always lose."

"That, my dear Mr. Pelham, is because the winners write history," Stohrs said, and Remo saw him reach his index finger forward to touch a button on the arm of his chair. Needles, he knew, would shoot up now into Remo's forearm, drugging him, putting him under.

How many had they done it to? Had they ever done it to a man who could respond quickly enough to pluck flies from the air between thumb and forefinger? It had come down to this: to Remo Williams and his terrible talents, against this evil man, this evil product of monstrous wrongs.

Stohrs' hand squeezed over the end of the chair. Remo focussed his perception on his right forearm. He felt the pinpricks against his skin. The act seemed frozen in slow motion. First, the three needles touched the skin. The skin bent before them like a marshmallow refusing a stick. The

174

needles insisted. Then the skin collapsed and gave way, surrounding the tips of the needles. The needles should now continue into the arm and give their narcotic juices. Then the victim should react by rubbing his arm.

That was the script for a victim. But Remo Williams was in the chair and he was no man's victim. His arm rose imperceptibly, then yanked away and he rubbed the inside of the right forearm. He felt slightly woozy and increased the speed of his body rhythms to absorb what could only have been a trace dose. His head sank forward onto his chest.

"So you will beat me, will you?," he heard Stohrs say. Stohrs' chair slid back from the table. Remo could hear him walking around toward him. He was a doctor. He would look into Remo's eyes. Lids closed tightly, Remo focussed his eyes on a jet plane in the sky of his imagination, miles away. He felt the practiced thumb press his eyelid up. The sudden light should have contracted the pupil. But the jet plane in that bright noon sky had already done that and Stohrs let the eyelid drop with a grunt of satisfaction.

"He's under," Stohrs yelled. "I'm keeping my promise to you."

"Stand up," he told Remo. It was a command and Remo stood. "Open your eyes and follow me." With confident arrogance, Stohrs turned his back on Remo and walked away. He pulled aside a long velvet drape, exposing a door. He turned the knob and walked in, stepping aside to let Remo pass.

Remo's eyes were fixed straight ahead, but his peripheral vision swallowed the room in a glance. He had seen the room before. In the sex photos. A metal bed stood against the left wall, covered with white satin sheets. At the right side of the small room stood a camera on a tripod, and reflector-covered lights. Behind the bed stood Anna. Her chest heaved, disturbing the fabric of her sweater as she looked at Remo. "I've waited for you a long time," she said.

Stohrs pushed the door shut and locked it. "Take off your clothes," he commanded. "All of them." Remo mechanically removed his clothes, watching straight ahead as Anna pulled her sweater off over her head, her blonde locks splashing through with difficulty. Her pendulous breasts bounced when released from the sweater. She returned Remo's stare as she reached behind her and snapped loose the top button of her skirt, hooked her fingers inside the waistband and slid it slowly down over her hips, until it dropped soundlessly on the floor. She wore no undergarments, only long black stockings, held up with a black garter belt, and black patent leather boots that reached above the knee.

Remo was naked, his clothes in a pile on the floor in front of him. "Lie on the bed," Stohrs ordered and Remo sprawled across the cot on his back. Anna walked to the bed alongside him, and leaned over him, the nipples of her breasts just touching his bare chest. "I have something special for you," she said. She stepped to a small table alongside the bed, then back into Remo's view. She held a black wig in her hands. She trailed the long strands of hair across Remo's stomach, his genitals, then down his legs. Then she placed it on her head, tucking her blonde hair under it.

She sat on the bed next to Remo and took a tube of lipstick from the table. She slid the end of the closed lipstick into her mouth, then leaned over Remo and let spittle from her mouth dribble onto his chest. Then she uncased the lipstick and painted deep red lips over her own pale color. She reached again for the table.

176

Now the whip, Remo thought.

Kill them now? It would be easy. But he wanted them to savor their victory, before he twisted it into death.

"Father, are you ready? I can no longer wait."

Stohrs, who had been loading the camera, said "Go ahead. But quickly. We have spent much time."

The whip now. It flashed expertly across Remo's stomach and snapped a red welt into his skin. Again. This time closer to his maleness. And again. Then she dropped the whip across the bed, and lowered her head over Remo. The dark strands of hair played across his body, and then she was on him, greasy lipstick working on him, moaning with passion.

Remo allowed himself to respond. He wanted this woman. Not to enjoy her. But to punish her. He had learned the secrets from Chiun. This twisted Nazi beast was infatuated by a husky young policeman, but she was going to be destroyed by the surrogate for an eighty-year old Korean who believed that women were no more complicated than guitars. The wrong strings produced disharmony. It is simply a matter of plucking the right strings.

The strings for the blackhaired woman in boots were pain and suffering and torture. That was her enjoyment. Remo would give her that until she was in ecstasy, and then give her more until the ecstasy turned to pain, and more yet until the soft erotic touch became the bitter rasp of a rawl.

Her voluntary act of debasement was lighting the fires.

"He's ready. Tell him to take me."

"Take her," Stohrs said.

"I want rape," yelled the daughter.

"Rape the woman," Stohrs said.

And that was all Remo needed, and he banged her down into the bed so hard that her wig flew off and

177

plowed into her, twisting her body so that her spinal column wrenched.

She moaned and Stohrs kept snapping pictures. What process had brought him to this, Remo thought, where he could stand taking photos and living out his daughter's perversions? Remo knew. It was like any other horror. It was done imperceptibly, step by step, individual meaningless actions being built into the habit pattern, demanding compliance, until the final act . . . the final sum . . . was demanded by the parts. Until there was no way to stop it.

"Harder." Anna's voice insinuated itself into his mind. Harder. Faster. Deeper. He considered his fingers. Then his toes. While his body forced blood to pump, his mind denied that blood and thought of other parts, other functions. It was Chiun's secret.

"More," she yelled. "More."

He ground into her, pressing with his knees, lifting her and dropping her down. She groaned in ecstasy.

Remo moved harder. Faster.

She groaned. Ecstasy again.

Harder. Faster. Concentrate on kneecaps.

She groaned continuously now. But ecstasy was giving way. It was surrendering to pain.

Remo moved on. Harder. Faster. His mind sensed the heavily calloused skin on the tips of his fingers.

Her groans grew in intensity, raised in pitch. She was in pain now. Suffering. She would soon shout *stop* and Remo, under drugs, would have to obey.

He leaned forward heavily onto her body and smashed his heavily muscled shoulder down into her mouth, chipping her front teeth. Hard. Stopping her from calling out the command to stop.

Her voice was muffled under his shoulder.

178

And Remo kept on. Harder. Harder. The toes now. He felt them digging into the wooden floor for a firm footing. She was using her hands now. Trying to push him away. He pressed her harder.

Stohrs had stopped taking pictures. He was now just a spectator. The Nazis had killed by gang rape. Stohrs was watching that fate overtake his daughter, a death administered by a one-man gang.

Then Stohrs called out. "Stop."

Remo stopped. And the bitch lay semi-conscious, bleeding from the mouth and groin.

"Are you all right, dear?," Stohrs asked.

She sat up slowly, hatred in her eyes. "Let us kill this bastard, father. Painfully."

"We shall. But first, Mr. Pelham and I must finish our game. Develop the film. I will call you."

Remo was ordered to dress, and then Stohrs led him back to the chess room. He ordered Remo to sit down and then took his seat on the other side of the table.

He spoked to Remo: "Who are you?"

"Remo Pelham."

"Who told you about me?"

"Deborah Hirshbloom."

"What did she tell you?"

"That you were Nazi."

"Why did you come here?"

"For money. I could get money from you."

"All right. We will play a little game. You will wake up and show me how you can win, and then you will go back to sleep. Repeat after me. You will wake up to play the game and then you will go to sleep."

"I will wake up to play and then go back to sleep."

"Back to sleep when I snap my fingers. Wake up when I snap my fingers."

And Stohrs snapped his fingers.

"A fast game," he said, smiling.

"A fast game," Remo said.

"Still think you can win?," Stohrs asked, confident in his skills, assured of his victory.

"Yes," Remo said. He picked up the queen from the board. Deborah's queen. "Watch the queen," Remo said.

"I am watching."

"It is my move," Remo said, as he lifted the queen, standing it on its green felt base in the palm of his hand. His fingers curled down to hold it by the base, against his palm. Then his deep brown eyes that seemed to have no pupils burned into Stohrs' eyes and Remo said, "It is mate in one." Remo turned the queen over in the palm of his right hand, and then, with a roll of the wrist, moved it forward. His move, the greatest move in the history of chess, put the white point into Stohr's right eye, and then a push through the socket into the brain, and there was Stohrs with a green felt monocle where his right eye should be, and red ribbons beginning to hang from it. Stohrs' body twitched convulsively and his fingers went snap, snap, snap, because that was the last message his brain had sent before Remo had moved, white queen to the bastard's eye.

Remo looked at him, then smiled with only his lips.

"Checkmate," he said. And walked away.

The rest was easy.

CHAPTER TWENTY-FOUR

Anna Stohrs was still naked. She was just placing the negatives of Remo into a metal card file containing the other negatives when Remo walked into the darkroom.

She looked up, and her eyes opened wide in horror, when she saw him there.

"He lost," Remo said.

She tried to kick him but Remo, laughing, ignored the effort, and flipped her left arm up behind her back. Then he whispered into her right ear, "Your father said just before I killed him that the one thing he really enjoyed was seeing you perform. But he never wanted to let on, because you might stop."

Then he killed her and left her body sprawled over the giant photo dryer. The sweat on her naked body sizzled as he dropped her over the stainless steel drum. Then Remo burned the negatives, and set fire to the house.

He took a doughnut from the cupboard on his way out, and left a few minutes before the arrival of the first fire company.

The cool of evening chilled the air, and suddenly it became incredibly cold for August, then hot, then Remo felt nothing and just kept walking.

CHAPTER TWENTY-FIVE

The roast beef at Henrici's in Dayton was good. It had been good for the last two Wednesday nights and Remo looked out of the windows down on the Miami valley, with blinking lights on the outskirts of Dayton, and farther off the small towns surrounding it. The restaurant was on the top of the hotel and for Dayton provided exquisite dining. In New York, it would be just another good meal.

He cut into the rich red beef, which shivered slightly, emitting a reddish pool which flowed into the mashed potato mountain, making its base pink. Good beef, someone had once said, was like a hearty woman. It must be taken with gusto. Who said it? It obviously had not been Chiun, who while he once allowed that all women are beautiful but not all men are capable of seeing it, also felt that red beef was like a subtle poison. You enjoyed your destruction because it was comfortable and slow.

Remo enjoyed the beef. In fact, Chiun might be very bright about the poison. Being some place at a certain night regularly, a certain place someone else knew, made you a perfect setup for that someone else. The beef could be poisoned. He could be poisoned without his poisoner ever seeing him. CURE was good at that. In fact, if it wanted to, the poisoner might not even know it was poison. Breaking links wherever you can.

But he was alive and every day he lived probably meant that he was being kept there to stew. The punishment would be waiting to be killed. If he waited, though, it would also show them that he could be trusted again.

What had he really done that was so bad? Talked back? That could be attributed to the long peak. What counted was not what he said but what he did. And what he did was to follow orders. He had headed for Deborah's cottage and then he went to Dayton.

How he had gotten to Dayton, he forgot. There was the path, the tiredness, the oppressive heat, and then, what he remembered of it, he was in the Dayton Airport just outside Vandalia, with an incredible sunburn, money from what must have been cashed traveler's checks and no identification. He had probably gone through the necessary go routine automatically.

He had noticed how weak he had become, but the rest improved him daily. When he returned to training, he would be well ready for it. But he would never again allow them to keep him at that level. He would explain this if he ever got to Smith again.

Deborah, of course, had gotten her man. He knew she would, but it was a sloppy job. He had heard about it in a bar. Father-daughter fight. But why would the woman choose suicide by photo-drying? Funny, it sounded like something he might do. The Israelis were supposed to be a bit neater. Yeah, he might do it. No, it just wasn't fast enough. For punishment, it would do. But Remo, however, was not in the punishment business.

Some day, if they should ever meet, he would tell Deborah how sloppy she had been.

He looked out over the valley, gazing for miles. It was a clear night, yet there were no stars, and for reasons he could not fathom, he felt deeply lost, as if he had found something so necessary to his life, then lost it without knowing what it was.

It was then that Remo created an original line of sentiment and felt proud of it. He thought of Deborah's freckles and said to himself, waiting to use it publicly to advantage some day, "A girl without freckles is like a night without stars."

Remo looked around the restaurant for a woman with freckles. He had to try out his original line. He saw only a man in a suit with a briefcase. The reason he saw only this was that the man was standing three inches from him.

"Enjoying yourself? Pleasant thoughts?" asked the man. It was a bitter thin voice. Remo looked up. It belonged to a bitter, hateful face.

"Good evening. Sit down. I wondered why you kept me waiting so long."

Remo watched Harold W. Smith take the other side of the table. He put his briefcase on his lap.

Smith ordered a grilled cheese sandwich. The waitress said, "We have something with tomatoes and bacon and. . . ."

"Just grilled cheese," he said.

"And make it unpleasant," Remo added. Ah, the waitress had freckles. He would devastate her.

The waitress hid a smile from all but the corner of her mouth.

"Be off," Smith said to the girl, and turning to Remo said: "My, you're in fine fettle. Did you enjoy yourself on your last business trip?"

185

"Not really."

"I never knew you liked to freelance."

"What?" Remo looked confused.

"You've forgotten little details?"

"I don't know what you mean."

Smith leaned over the table and peered intently at Remo's forehead, where his peeled skin was still taut and shiny, and his eyebrows were just growing back.

"Well, the reports said it was there, so I suppose I'll buy it. And I do have Chiun's explanation."

"Buy what?" Smith smiled and Remo knew that he was not supposed to ask.

"When did you recover your memory? I mean fully?"

"Tell you what," Remo said, "you tell me how I got this sunburn because I'm sure you know and I'll tell you when I recovered my memory."

"You'll tell me when you recovered your memory."

"At the Dayton Airport."

"That's about right," Smith said. He looked around him and said, lest anyone be listening, "You left your wallet in my room this morning." He handed Remo a well-worn wallet containing, as Remo knew, who he would be and where he would go and what he should look for that would tell him where he would meet Smith again.

"What about the sunburn?"

"Someday ask Chiun. I can't even understand it, much less be able to explain it."

Smith surveyed the fine surroundings and added: "You know, if the tables weren't so close together, I'd like to see you eating the next time in an automat."

"You would," said Remo, placing his wallet and new self in the pocket of the new suit he had bought for cash.

The waitress was back, putting the grilled cheese sandwich in front of Smith.

"You know," Remo said as she bent over, "a girl without freckles is like a night without stars."

"I know," she said. "My boyfriend tells me that."

And Smith took obvious delight in Remo's obvious deflation.

"I swear it," Remo said to Smith. "There is not an original line in the world. Whatever you make up has been made up before. I had made that up. It was mine."

"Rubbish," said Smith with the quiet contentment of seeing another soul return from the clouds to the daily level of discontent. "A mutual friend of ours used to use it all the time. Little girls, old women, anyone he could bamboozle. When he was sober enough to talk."

And Remo, who knew whom Smith was talking about, dropped his fork in the potatoes and said, with thorns of outrage, "I remember every word that guy ever said to me. And he never told me that."

"If you say so," said Smith biting into the yellow goo of his sandwich.

And Remo leaned back. "I don't care if you don't believe me. At least I know I have poetry in my heart. You know. Heart, sensitivity, people, human beings."

He did not now feel like eating and he watched the Miami valley, the moving lights of the cars, the dots of lights that were far-off homes.

"All right. I really believe you made that up originally. It's possible. Now finish your dinner. We're paying for it."

Remo continued to look out into the dark waiting for a similar inspiration to come to him so he could prove himself on the point. But the inspiration was not there.

THE EXECUTIONER

The most exciting series ever to explode into print!

Meet Mack Bolan, self-appointed one-man death squad sworn to destroy the Mafia—single-handed! Stung by his devastating attacks, the Families have put out a $100,000 contract on him, and every gun man in the world is welcome to try to collect on it! Bolan is alone, as even the forces of law and order are out to stop his solitary killer crusade.

You won't want to miss a single word of this dynamite series. Check the order form on the last page and get your copies today!

THE BEST IN PAPERBACKS FROM PINNACLE BOOKS!

If you enjoyed this book, you're sure to want the other exciting titles from PINNACLE BOOKS. Here are the highlights of the most intriguing and entertaining paper back books being published today!

ORDER NOW TO KEEP AHEAD!

To order, check the space next to the books you want, then mail your order, together with cash, check or money order, to: Pinnacle Books, Mail Order Dep't., Box 4347, Grand Central Station, New York, New York 10017.

Order No.	Title	Price
___P003	CATACLYSM, The Day The World Died	95¢
___P004	THE EXECUTIONER'S BATTLE MASK	95¢
___P005	BLOOD PATROL	95¢
___P006	THE GUNS OF TERRA 10	95¢
___P007	1989: POPULATION DOOMSDAY	95¢
___P008	MIAMI MASSACRE	95¢
___P009	KILLER PATROL	95¢
___P010	THE GODMAKERS	95¢
___P011	KILL QUICK OR DIE	95¢
___P012	CAST YOUR OWN SPELL	95¢
___P013	THE VEGAS TRAP	95¢
___P014	THE FEMINISTS	95¢
___P015	THE DEAD SEA SUBMARINE	95¢
___P016	STAY YOUNG WITH ASTROLOGY	95¢
___P017	THE EXECUTIONER: CONTINENTAL CONTRACT	95¢
___P018	TALKING TO THE SPIRITS	95¢
___P019	THE AVENGER TAPES	$1.25
___P020	TO CATCH A CROOKED GIRL	95¢
___P021	THE DEATH MERCHANT	95¢
___P022	THE GREAT STONE HEART	95¢
___P023	THE DEADLY SKY	95¢
___P024	THE DAY THE SUN FELL	$1.25
___P025	COME WATCH HIM DIE	95¢
___P026	SLATER'S PLANET	95¢
___P027	HOME IS WHERE THE QUICK IS: MOD SQUAD #	95¢
___P028	EVERYTHING YOU NEED TO KNOW ABOUT ABORTION	$1.50
___P029	THE EXECUTIONER: ASSAULT ON SOHO	95¢
___P030	OPERATION RESCUE	$1.25
___P031	THE US. GOVERNMENT BUDGET COOKBOOK	95¢
___P032	TALES OF HORROR AND THE SUPERNATURAL, VOLUME ONE	95¢
___P033	FLIGHT OF HAWKS	95¢
___P034	PARADISE IS NOT ENOUGH	95¢
___P035	TERROR IN RIO	95¢
___P036	OTHER SIDE OF THE CLOCK	95¢
___P037	THE ESCAPE ARTIST	95¢
___P038	CREATED THE DESTROYER	95¢

___	P039	THE EXECUTIONER, War Against The Mafia	95¢
___	P040	THE EXECUTIONER'S DEATH SQUAD	95¢
___	P041	LOVE SONG	$1.25
___	P042	THE NEW COOK'S COOKBOOK	$1.25
___	P043	THE ALIEN EARTH	95¢
___	P044	THE EXECUTIONER: NIGHTMARE IN NEW YORK	95¢
___	P046	THE RECTOR	95¢
___	P047	LOVE AMERICAN STYLE	95¢
___	P048	THE SPRINGING OF GEORGE BLAKE	$1.50
___	P049	THE BELLS OF WIDOW'S BAY	95¢
___	P050	IMPERIAL TRAGEDY	$1.95
___	P051	THE EXECUTIONER: CHICAGO WIPEOUT	95¢
___	P052	THE GOLDEN OYSTER	95¢
___	P053	DAUGHTER OF HENRY VIII	95¢
___	P054	TALES FROM THE UNKNOWN	95¢
___	P055	CIVIL WAR II	95¢
___	P056	FOURTH STREET EAST	$1.25
___	P057	HOW TO MARRY A MARRIED MAN	95¢
___	P058	THE GROUPSEX SCENE	$1.25
___	P059	THE EXECUTIONER: VEGAS VENDETTA	95¢
___	P060	THE VALIANT SAILORS	95¢
___	P061	SABERLEGS	95¢
___	P062	FIRST CONTACT	95¢
___	P063	TIMES AND PLACES	$1.25
___	P064	THE CLASH OF DISTANT THUNDER	95¢
___	P065	CALLEY: SOLDIER OR KILLER	95¢
___	P066	NAKED, AS AN AUTHOR	95¢
___	P067	GUNS FOR GENERAL LI	95¢
___	P069	THE PENTAGON	$1.95
___	P070	BRAVE CAPTAINS	95¢
___	P071	CONGO WAR CRY	95¢
___	P072	THE DESTROYER: DEATH CHECK	95¢
___	P073	101 BEST GROWTH STOCKS FOR 1972	$1.25
___	P074	DUELING OAKS	95¢
___	P090	BURN AFTER READING	95¢
___	P092	HOW TO "MAKE IT" 365 DAYS A YEAR	$1.25

Pinnacle Books, Box 4347, Grand Central Station, New York, New York 10017

Gentlemen:
  Please send me the books I have marked. I enclose

$_____as payment in full. (Sorry, no CODs.)

Name_____

Address_____

City_____State_____Zip_____